The Black Land

MJ WESOLOWSKI

BLOOD BOUND BOOKS

Copyright © 2013 by MJ Wesolowski
All rights reserved

ISBN 978-1-940250-07-6

Artwork by Richard Andrew Disley

Printed in the United States of America

First Edition

Visit us on the web at:
www.bloodboundbooks.net

Also from Blood Bound Books:

400 Days of Oppression by Wrath James White

Loveless by Dev Jarrett

The Sinner by K. Trap Jones

Mother's Boys by Daniel I. Russell

Knuckle Supper by Drew Stepek

Sons of the Pope by Daniel O'Connor

Dolls by KJ Moore

At the End of All Things by Stony Graves

The Return by David A. Riley

For Nora and Harry Barfoot – *The seas called you home.*

First there was the whale-road, and there was nothing more.

Then, from this whale's-way rose the land.

And from the land came the riders of the sea-steeds.

Their serpent heads dipped like song into the waves, lip to lip with the daughters of Ægir they sailed until they struck land.

Their land.

The dark men aboard the wave horse held aloft their shields and claimed the island for their own.

For their hanged god spoke to them, his lip steams spun through rock and stone, Blamenholm was theirs.

And in the name of their spear master, they would never leave.

.

The whir of the helicopter was a deafening, steady thrum above the hiss and crash of waves hurling themselves against the rocks. A light but permeating swell of rain descended from the black cloud that had rolled over the horizon and darkened the morning.

Inside the helicopter's squat capsule, the Walker family stared eagerly out at the land below, their excited exclamations communicated in the buzzing, clipped tones of their headsets as the Bell 407 began its descent onto the barren grass of the island that seemed to be rising from the expanse of sea below them. The kids had tried to christen the place "Dad's Island" but the name wouldn't quite stick. Its true title, Blamenholm, stood defiant, almost stubborn in the face of their attempted trivialization.

There was a silence inside the craft as the family waited for the blades to stop turning and the pilot gave the all clear for them to exit. Up ahead, through the rain-spattered front window, the castle could be made out; a gray, cuboid structure with slim, black windows that gazed up at them in a spectral leer. Unlike its peers in Bamburgh or Alnwick, the castle could never be described as beautiful. There were no Georgian gardens, nor plush visitor center. The only alterations to the place that seemed in any way modern were the chains and faded signage that clung to the castle's outer gate in front of the warped chipboard that had been hastily nailed over the doorway. Lichen and moss clung to the wall that enclosed the main drive of the castle and only its upper floors could be seen from ground level, glaring over the wall at the visitors. No trees stood on the island; its only flora, alongside the lichen, were the white tendrils of scurvy grass and stunted ragwort.

Even the yellow flowers that shone from the peat of the Farne Islands nature reserve that lay some miles behind were absent here.

Martin Walker, resplendently coifed and surrounded by a faint tang of Ralph Lauren, had his hand on the inner handle of the helicopter hatch. He revolved his proud smile around the cabin, meeting the eyes of his wife and children as they gazed from him to the sight that greeted them. Martin nodded at the pilot's thumbs up when a voice came from the far corner of the cabin.

"Careful where you walk, there are fissures on Blamenholm that will swallow a man whole."

Martin stopped and stared around at the man perched lackadaisically on one of the seats, still staring out at the rain that peppered the windows of the helicopter. He had a thick thatch of jet black curls above a rounded, weather-beaten face. His sharp, brown eyes darted all around the tight cabin of the helicopter, his visage not unlike some tattered bird of prey. Procured after weeks of searching, dressed in a worn, black greatcoat and crumpled army boots, this was their guide to the island.

"Sorry, Saul," Martin said, grinning. "Do you want to do the honors?"

Saul turned to face the family, running a hand through his mane of curls, making them stand up as he smiled back.

"Of course," he intoned. This guy had an English accent, not exactly Dick Van Dyke, more Ian McKellen—Gandalf was the name that simultaneously sprung into Chad and Lauren Walker's minds, unbeknownst to each other.

Saul slid from his seat and pulled open the door of the helicopter, letting in the freezing, salt-tinged wind.

He hopped, cat-like out onto the land, his boots squelching on the muddy peat.

→⌐

The majority of the time Martin Walker had spent in the North East of England before the family had flown out had been largely frustrating.

Closing the deal on acquiring the castle, hell, the whole island of Blamenholm had felt like a damn snipe hunt. Martin first had to find its owner, a guy called Sage who apparently held the title of "Lord."

Martin was not naive enough to believe that all English nobility lived in Buckingham-style palaces, or were revered by their subjects who lined their driveways waving little Union Jacks, but the completely opposite reaction to the mention of Lord Sage was disconcerting. He began in Alnwick, the largest and most accessible of the small towns in the area, but he was faced with blank stares at the mention of Sage's name in every tourist information center and shop. Eventually, directed by a hand-drawn map on the back of a receipt by one of the ancient volunteers at Alnwick library, Martin Walker and his Gateway Resorts team ended up thirty five miles north in the tiny parish of Chillingham, at the door of a retired policeman's tall manor, hidden from the road by a platoon of looming poplars.

"Lord Sage. That's not a name I've cared to remember for thirty years," sniffed the man who had eventually opened the door. His voice was a dry croak.

Beaming his family-man-done-good smile, Martin had stepped forward and taken the old man's withered hand in his own, feeling thin fingers, like the brittle bones of chicken beneath roasted skin.

"Sir," he said, displaying perfect rows of white teeth. "You could be a huge help to me."

"Bell's me name." The old man looked back up at Martin, his eyes turning skyward, showing their yellowy corners. "And divvint you try that charm shit with me, son, I was in the force all my life, and I've seen it all before."

Martin had been shocked for a second at the way Bell had looked past his façade with such ease. A policeman never really stops being a policeman, he supposed. Then he laughed, loud, leaning back. The sound of it in the silent afternoon sent a few birds flapping from the nearby trees.

"Lord Sage isn't a popular subject round here, like," Bell said after a long silence following Martin's explanation of their predicament. "Never was, never will be."

Martin made to move forward, expecting to be invited in and sit through a long, tiresome story. From what he'd picked up around the area, Lord Sage had been somewhat of an unconventional "Lord," keeping to himself and never leaving his island. The small town rumors began in the late fifties and early sixties, drugs, witchcraft yadda-yadda-yadda. The guy was probably just a bit of an eccentric old hippie who did not want every Tom, Dick, and Harry traipsing round his property with all their snot-nosed kids in tow.

But Bell did not budge. He glared up at Martin; the quiet in this odd little place was disconcerting, almost creepy to a guy who was used to the constant roar of traffic and the thrum of business.

"I'll give you directions," Bell croaked, his throat puffing out as he fumbled in his cardigan pocket for a pair of spectacles, "to where I think he is now. I assume all this is about Blamenholm, yes?"

4

Martin nodded. That was the policeman again, reading him like a book.

"You don't want owt to do with that place." Bell backed away after scribbling down an address. He pulled the door closed with a tremble in his hand. He spoke his last words through the slim gap before he clicked his front door shut, "And neither do I. Don't come back here. You hear me?"

A bemused Martin and his team eventually tracked down Lord Sage in a nursing home even further north in the border town of Berwick-Upon-Tweed. Just like in Alnwick and Chillingham, the staff were tight-lipped to the point of obstinacy about the man. Was it his title? Was it merely the fact that he was a lord and if a lord did not want to be found, there were people who'd be happy to oblige?

For a price, of course.

But money also opened doors, and eventually a grim-faced Eastern European woman led the team up a narrow flight of stairs to the very top of the home. The idea of this guy as a "Lord" was deflating with each step up the faded carpet and peeling wallpaper, with each scent of nostril-clenching chemicals over a light undertone of human feces. When they reached Sage's room and pushed open the door, Martin couldn't even remember the term "Lord" applied to this guy. His room in the home was completely bare, not even a photograph adorned his bedside table.

The hunched, almost skeletal fellow was ninety years old in a pair of standard-issue pajamas and, as they were told by the staunch woman who'd led them here, was silenced by Alzheimer's. He did not even look round when they entered the room.

For weeks, he did not utter a single word to the representatives from Gateway, it was only when Martin had just about given up and paid a solitary visit to the lonely room to admit defeat that Sage had handed him a letter. It was written in a shaking, nearly illegible script, specifying that all transactions would go through his only surviving relative, Saul, who would show them around the castle before they made a final decision.

"I kinda *have* made the decision, sir..." Martin Walker had said, but the old man had simply looked at him, his sunken blue eyes widening before he turned away, his head shaking.

"I kinda *have to* make this decision, now, sir," he amended, voice louder this time with a slight tremor of desperation.

Had the old man heard it? He placed his hands over his face and began to sob into his hands, his bony shoulders high, like the stumps of wings.

The nurse on duty had indicated that Martin should leave, but when his hands touched the doorknob, he was sure he had heard muttered words burbling through the sobs from Sage, who stood trembling beside his long window.

"Home," it sounded like. "Get home."

Martin trusted his intuition. Always had, always would.

He heard it now, he knew what it said. What it almost screamed.

But they could not go home.

⌐⌐

The Walker family now stood beneath the shadow of Blamenholm's outer gate, hoods pulled up and cheeks red from the wind. Saul stood in front of them, his back to the chains and coils of rusted barbed wire that hung from the top of the walls like some long-dead coil of

6

ivy. He was gazing at the upturned faces of the Walker children who were strangely quiet, as if in awe of the looming structure before them, his eyes playful.

"Let's just imagine for a second," Saul said, a smile on the corners of his lips, "this island back in the year seven hundred and ninety three."

He looked away, into the distance for a second, almost as if he had heard some voice in the roar of the ocean.

"Imagine you're a monk." The children looked at him, slightly puzzled, and he said, "Bald guys, big on God, did lots of writing, reading and not a lot else." Saul's eyes twinkled.

"Swore celibacy too, those guys," Martin said, smirking.

His voice seemed loud and obtrusive, his attempt at humor torn away by the wind and scattered to the rocks as his wife Martha and daughter Lauren glanced at each other, wearing matching scowls of irritation.

"What's celibacy?" Chad, Martin's youngest, piped up.

Martha pulled a "there you go" expression at her husband and Martin sighed, his expression darkening. He waved his wife's look from him with a flick of his fingers and a twitch of his nose.

A tight silence fell.

"Did you ever hear of Vikings?" Saul said, suddenly, his eyes snapping back to the children.

Both Chad and Lauren took in sharp little intakes of breath, their attention snapping back to Saul's shaggy countenance.

"They came in dragon-headed longboats from the north." He pointed to the sullen, cloud-filled horizon. The Walker children followed his gaze.

Lauren nodded but stayed silent, a twitch of annoyance at getting caught out on her face. Chad gazed at Saul, enraptured.

"I've heard of Vikings, sir," Chad said, proudly.

"Imagine seeing those boats from these islands," Saul continued, his voice grave, "imagine seeing your death riding high upon those waves and there being no escape."

Martha Walker looked to her husband, concern in her eyes, but Martin placed a finger to his lips.

"Fearsome warriors from Sweden, Iceland, Norway." Saul was speaking almost to himself before looking back at the children. "Killing, burning, pillaging." Saul's voice was grim. "They were just men, you see…"

The wind was picking up now, and foamy, white heads of waves were increasing on the slate blue of the North Sea that roared around the island.

"Did the monks not fight back?" Chad asked in a quiet, sober tone.

"Have you ever heard of a *berserker*?" Saul smiled again, but this time it was a wistful, almost sad expression.

"Like in 'Gears of War?'" Chad exclaimed.

Lauren gave her little brother a withering look. "They were *warriors*, dummy," she said, crossing her arms over her chest. "Or something."

"Exactly!" Saul extended one of his long fingers and pointed at Lauren, whose cheeks reddened as she turned shyly to her left.

"The Norsemen called them *Úlfhéðnar*, 'wolf-skins.'" His face slipped swiftly from a smile back to seriousness. "Imagine." He lowered his finger and looked again into the black scowl of the sky. "Imagine men who feel no pain, who will cleave through friend

8

and foe alike. Men who charge into battle clothed in the skins of fearsome wolves, their mouths foaming with bloodlust."

"Wolf-men," Chad whispered, his eyes wide.

"Aw, c'mon." Martha Walker murmured, pressing her forehead to her husband's sodden shoulder.

"Honey, please," Martin said. "This guy's a pro! It's good for them! It's educational."

Martha sighed, turning her own eyes to the heavens. The rain kept up its constant rattle against their waterproof coats and the cries of seabirds echoed mournfully across the wind.

"The Norsemen who garrisoned here sacked the abbey at Lindisfarne and burned it to the ground," Saul's voice was suddenly booming, solemn, like that of a preacher. "Legend says there was a place somewhere in the keep, where they could awaken the berserkers. That they lost their minds, that they became 'berserk' in the fortress of Blamenholm."

The Walkers looked to each other with wide, excited eyes. Chad mouthed "Cool" to his father, whose face was a goofy, childish grin.

"What do you mean, they became berserk?" Lauren's tone was scornful. "That doesn't make any sense."

"Shut up!" Chad whined, turning around to glare at his sister with an almost hysterical fury. "Why do you have to ruin everything?"

"Whatever." Lauren grunted, rolling her eyes.

"Kids!" Martha raised her hands to her mouth in shock. "Just. *Stop*. Okay?"

Sure, siblings fought, hadn't she fought with her own array of older sisters who shirked on their chores and blamed Martha, tucking away knowing smiles behind blank faces as the wrath of their mother seemed to shake the whole house? Chad and Lauren though, this was just not them.

"Honey." Martin, ever the diplomat, spread his arms and stepped forward between the two children who were glaring at each other. Martha felt her toes curl at his curt dismissal of her.

"Chad, Lauren." Martin stared at his kids for a few seconds until their heads dropped. "I know we're all excited to see Daddy's castle, but let's just keep it cool, huh?"

He turned his winning smile on Saul, who, throughout this small debacle, had been staring worriedly up at the grey wall that seemed to loom at an angle over them, its shadow cradling them in its square darkness.

"I must apologize, they've never really seen stuff like this before, not back home, and you know—*kids*."

Saul shook himself from his reverie and smiled back warmly but slightly uncomprehending, like someone who does not quite understand the language spoken.

"No apologies necessary," he said. "The Sages themselves found the castle had a most profound effect on their temperament when they were its residents."

Saul jumped at the sudden shriek of a sea bird, a colossal herring gull that burst from somewhere above them in the castle walls, cawing furiously and beating the air with its disconcertingly wide wingspan before disappearing away across the sea. The Walker family moved together again slightly and Saul cleared his throat.

"What were we saying? Berserkers. Yes. Well, many believe that berserkers were members of what we would call a *cult* these days, the 'Children of Odin' they called themselves."

The gulls yelped from somewhere high in the castle's walls, the sea hissed against the rocks.

"Clothed in masks and the skins of wolves or bears, these men would dance long into their night as homage to their one-eyed war god."

"Crazy," Lauren whispered. Saul looked up.

"Not crazy but *high*."

Lauren suppressed a smirk.

"*Amanita muscaria*," Saul said with a flourish, "or hallucinogenic toadstool to you and me. It used to grow all over the island. No idea how, but it did. The berserkers would gorge themselves on the stuff and dance themselves into a frenzy—no wonder they felt no pain."

Saul turned and produced a bunch of keys from his greatcoat pockets and fumbled with the chains that held the gate of the castle closed.

"That's where the island gets its name, you see," Saul said as the rusted metal chains chuckled gutturally in his hands. "The *Blámmen* are the 'black men,' the berserkers... the demons."

The gate of Blamenholm castle finally opened with a painful squeal from the long-rusted hinges.

With an almost unnoticeable trepidation, the Walker family followed Saul inside.

2

Martin Walker had opened his first Gateway resort in the Ozarks in 1991 after six months of negotiation with investors and the bank. He had attended the building site deep in the Black River forest and worked daily 12-hour shifts during its first year of opening. The result of this passion resulted in a luxurious holiday destination that's exclusivity made it profitable in its first year. Since then, Martin had opened several more Gateways across the wild areas of the United States and stood back as the money rolled in.

The thing that distinguished the Gateways from the thousands of similar wilderness resorts was the guarantee of total isolation, privacy, and above all, luxury. No expense was spared on the open-plan, self-contained cabins with their own land. State-of-the-art tinted glass ceilings, and wall-windows allowed guests to experience the majesty of the outdoors while staying warm, dry, and watching satellite television on huge flat-screens in mezzanine bedrooms. Food, towels, and toiletries were delivered using a touchscreen in each cabin from a central hub, equidistant from each cabin.

Lucrative deals were made with adventure companies, a Gateway customer could book a white-water rafting, horseback riding or off road biking experience at no extra cost. Not only was Gateway an instant success with the affluent and (sometimes) famous, it won an award for its sustainability and environmentally-friendly practices.

Following the success of his resorts, the life of his wife, Martha, and the two children was comfortably luxurious. They lived in a huge, gated ex-equestrian estate in Huntleigh, just outside St. Louis, complete with ivy-ensnared pergola and Pebble Tec pool. The children attended private schools, took riding and skiing lessons, and did not want for the latest clothes and electronics.

Martin Walker was, as he found the most effective way of putting it, all-in-all a family man made good. People loved that, it softened them up, gave him a way in. Sure, making good sometimes meant that he had to forego Martha's book launch, but what use was he there anyway? He could have stood, grinning as awkward-looking academics and chemistry majors stared through him as they gazed sycophantically at his wife—or he could be breaking deals in his board room, the warm crunch of his fist against the polished wood of his desk when he *closed that motherfucker* and felt the dollar signs rattling around his eyes like a crazed Scrooge McDuck on the 42-inch plasma he'd bought the Chadster after the little guy aced that spelling bee. He'd had the thing FedExed all the way from Dallas to surprise the kid when all the other guys' dads were taking them out for sodas. So he hadn't made it to the final, but Chad was never going to send the crowds wild at the Super Bowl, would never hear his name chanted by cheerleaders with long legs, and no one would look up from their tiered seats, beer and hotdogs in their hands at Chad's father with jealous adoration in their eyes. Yeah, maybe that dream was dead, but Chad had been taken on holidays that the other guys could only dream of. That was all that mattered.

Lauren had wanted her thirteenth at Burger King, but he wasn't going to sit and be ignored by a bunch of burger-munching teens, not if she wanted that darn horse or whatever she was always bugging him about.

Accommodation for the Walker family in the North East of England had been arranged at the last minute, when it became clear that the negotiations for Martin's new project were going to take longer than expected. However, Martin was confident. He didn't believe that flying his family out to see the place would *jinx* it or any of that bullshit. In fact, it would only make it seem more real. The island of Blamenholm had captured his imagination hook, line, and sinker. It had reached into his heart and clasped tight. When Martin thought of the island, he felt that familiar rushing sensation in his stomach he only felt when he was about to *close a motherfucker!* He wasn't a total dummy, however, he knew that some big ol' American guy staking his claim on one of England's ancient places wouldn't sit right in the stomachs of some. People hated progress, hadn't he found that out the goddamn hard way?

The people up here were as stony and gray as their damn weather. The Walkers would stay in a five-star converted mill, a few miles from the small, market town of Wooler, close to the coastline of the picturesque Northumbrian countryside. Martin's extensive Gateway entourage would be housed in a hotel, where he could also conduct business meetings without disturbing his family. He had personally filled the trunk of his car with food: fresh, succulent meat from the quaint little butchers shops where bells still jingled over the doors, juice and cereal from the not-so-quaint supermarkets whose automatic doors purred you inside. He roared along the winding A-roads and left it all in a basket on the mill's vast kitchen table. The smile on Martin's face as he sped through Northumberland never dissipated. He had that *feel*, that goddamned *feel*. This was going to work. One of the Gateway drivers would take Martha and the kids the hour or two's drive from the airport when they finally arrived in England. He would have done it himself, but there were places he needed to be. They were just going to love the place. He knew it.

Martha had been impressed as the car took them north, leaving behind the outlying suburbs of Newcastle-Upon-Tyne and entering the flat coastline of Northumberland. The kids looked pretty mesmerized through their jet lag. They did not speak, only stared at the still, yellow fields whizzing by as the road wound around tight corners and over the ridges and dips of the stark countryside. Something about the virtual absence of passers-by, farmers, folks on a day out echoed of the Nebraska plains of Martha Walker's childhood.

She could almost picture Uncle Karl's battered hay cart trundling along one of these roads, the bitter belch of his decrepit tractor billowing behind. As a girl, she had ridden on the hay cart many times, staring up at the endless blue of the sky while the hay's sharp fingers prodded the backs of her legs and neck, drawing squeaks and giggles from Martha and the other girls. On Halloween Uncle Karl would take Martha and her shrieking girlfriends through the trees of the nearby wood. It was only a copse, but she remembered the rows of trees, seemingly endless in the autumn darkness, the hay at their necks like the claws of a witch, the idea of the engine of the tractor sputtering out and Uncle Karl turning around, his face a pale skull.

Luckily, the children did not notice her start and shiver as she awoke, staring out at the now dim landscape. The day was nearly over, the sun was falling rapidly, casting a languid warmth across the land. From the right hand windows of the vehicle, the coastline was still visible, the fields fading into the pale green of sand dunes and the hard blue of the sea. To Lauren, this blue was different from the neat squares of swimming pools you could see when you reached the summit of one of the hills that rose behind the river back home (the view you'd see if you let some *boy* drive you up there to *look at the view*, which meant a stilted observation of how *small* everything looked before his hands were inside your bra). Windows, Lauren always thought of the pools. Pale, pointless, empty windows into nothing, whereas the slate blue of the fierce North Sea was *real*, unfathomable in its vast distance.

The Farne islands were visible on the tip of the horizon and the turrets of the castle at Bamburgh, perched on its high hill glowed almost orange in the wilting sunlight. Outside the car, the burble of wood pigeons and the rustle of the breeze were the only other noises on the quiet trickle of road. Inside, Chad was exhausted, done, curled into the corner of the car, his forehead casting a film of gray condensation on the window. There was so much to take in. Chad had never felt like he was on an island until now; a part of him imagined England to be almost miniature, just like home, but you know, smaller. The geography books he devoured at school painted a similar picture, but Lauren had snorted derisively on the plane when he'd speculated on whether they'd be able to see Big Ben from their bedroom when they got to the cottage. England was way bigger than he'd imagined.

The low voices of Lauren and her mother were only just audible alongside the roar of the car's engine and Chad's breathing.

"It's pretty, huh?"

Martha was expecting swift rebuttal from Lauren, whose teenage years were manifesting themselves in the inevitable outbursts of uncooperative pouting and flouncing. However, Lauren, drowsy but alert, was taking in the scenery with childish, wide-eyed fervor.

"It's *real* pretty, Mom, like something out of a story, you know?"

Martha smiled, seeing in Lauren's face both the woman she would become and the little girl she had been not so long ago. The jet lag and the quiet majesty of this alien country seemed to have combined, capturing Lauren's naturally inquisitive nature. Her iPod speakers lay redundant, coiled at her chest.

"There's a castle near here where they filmed *Harry Potter*." Martha smiled as her daughter's eyes widened further.

"And Dad's arranged for you and Chad to go on a boat ride tomorrow to those islands." She pointed out to the serene-looking crests of the sea.

"When do we get to see *Dad's* island?" Lauren asked, wriggling slightly in the seat to get more comfortable.

"In a few days, sweetie," Martha said, turning back to face the road.

"Mmm…" Lauren's eyes were closed now as the car rumbled on and the land ahead darkened.

3

"It stinks!" Chad Walker said, grasping his nostrils with a gloved hand.

The permeating, acrid stench of seabird droppings rent the air as the small boat began its approach to the tooth-like stacks of gray dolerite that jutted from the swaying water. The sound of the birds was relentless, the *scree, scree* of the back-hooded Terns and the yellow-beaked Kittiwakes that hurled their names against the ancient rock. Their droppings that coated the stacks of stone where the seabirds perched precariously on crumpled nests looked like pale frost on dark slate.

Chad was swaddled tight into a stiff raincoat and a red Berghaus fleece that still smelled of the shop; North Face or something like that, he didn't care, one of Dad's people had bought it. He had taken off his hat, letting the salt-crusted wind whip at his thin, blonde hair and the sea-fret spatter his face. The boat that carried them was riding the choppy waves of the North Sea, crashing forward, its nose lifting high into the air before colliding again and again with the surface of the water.

Lauren was sitting on the other side of the deck, scowl-down, tapping away at her phone... basically being Lauren. Being Lauren meant being the freaking Grinch twenty-four hours out of every day, stopping only to cackle over reality television or some meme that one of her Grinch friends had posted on Tumblr. It was no surprise the camaraderie between Chad and his big sis in the last year or so had ground to a halt, now grunts of *A-hole* and *retard* greeted even the most reasonable requests, y'know, for her to perhaps not bogart the entire bandwidth or for him to occasionally to use the TV. His *older* sister. Go figure.

Mom had bought Lauren's clothes in the same shop where Chad had his chosen for him: scarf, gloves, coat, hat and the boots that Lauren could not stop *whiiiinnnninnnggg about, cuz her feeeeeet huuuurrrrt and they were fuuuuuuugly*. Chad didn't gripe about the fact that, sure, they looked pretty dorky in their matching coats, but this wind was almost angry in its constant screeching against the sea and the coats kept its blade blunt. Lauren was supposed to be older. Right?

Dad was in "advanced negotiations" today, which basically translated as "gone." He'd have left before Chad even woke up and wouldn't be back till the pitch blackness of the countryside lay behind the curtains, till way after the screen of Chad's iPad became blurry and he had no choice but to close his eyes and let sleep take him.

Mom had come on the boat trip to the Farne Islands, but Chad knew for a fact she got sick on boats, despite her too-tight smile as they boarded the rickety little vessel at the rickety little port in the rickety little fishing village of Seahouses. The place was tiny, just like everywhere else here. Handfuls of toy cottages dotted the straw-colored sloping hills and clumps of tangled, picture-book trees. He wasn't sure about the others, except Dad of course, but Chad knew he *loved* it. Was love even the right word? Probably not. It was something else, something he just could not name. It was in the cry of the birds *Kitti-WAKE, kitti-WAKE* that beat inside his heart and the rush-roar of the sea that filled his head. It didn't matter about Lauren, she could stick to her grinching and Mom—Mom was hanging over the front of the ship, eyes to the sky and Chad bet a hundred dollars that she was smiling. Chad shifted his gaze to the rest of the boat's occupants, the two in grimy yellow oilskins who did not look back. Both men had dark, lined faces with skin that looked leathery and prematurely ancient. They spent their whole lives out in this wind. One had tried to talk to Chad after it was clear that Lauren was showing no interest whatsoever in the trip, but Chad could barely understand the man's accent.

"If ya luk oot, ya meyt see yersel' a *seel*, kidda!"

It probably wasn't a question, he hoped, but he smiled back a wide, friendly grin. He had no idea what any of it meant, but probably not a great idea to get ol' leatherface pissed at you on the very first day here, right?

The man had tried a few more times, "Divvint worry sunna, we're not gan far, y'knaa" and "Y'wanna be careful o'them geps gannin awa eh?," tapping the lens of Chad's glasses with a nicotine-stained finger, before giving up and wandering across the shallow deck to the little upright cabin where the boat's driver manned a dumb-looking plastic steering wheel. It looked like someone has just yanked it from a car and stuck it on a boat and started out to sea. Chad was sure he heard the men say something about "yanks" in a low, grouchy tone, but he chose to ignore them, instead, staring back out to see the hordes of shrieking birds that rose with the waves.

Chad knew for a stone-cold fact that if Dad had been on the boat with them, that these guys wouldn't be griping. They'd be all smiles, bending their backs to make sure the Walkers were okay. Hell, they might even offer Mom some old-time remedy for sea sickness rather than just leaving her to retch over the side. Dad had that effect on people, he always had; sometimes Chad didn't even think of him as Dad, not like a "Dad" dad… He didn't look like anyone else's dad. He was thin. "Trim" was how Mom described him, no beer gut spilling out of a stained Cardinals sweatshirt like some of the other slobs back home. He dressed well, too. Beige Lacoste and decent sneakers on his day off, a killer suit when he was working. "Dressed to kill" was how he liked to describe himself, with that great big grin on his face. In that way he wasn't like anyone else's dad, and was kinda cool.

The boat tour of the Farne Islands had been Dad's idea of course, only the best for you, kiddo. He had met them at Newcastle airport after their ten-hour flight from Lambert-St. Louis for an hour or so, before racing off to a meeting, and leaving them in the care of their hired driver. He had bought them tall, strong mugs of coffee and too-sweet muffins that had made Chad feel slightly sick. Lauren ate half and pushed the rest away in disgust. It was in the pale departure lounge of this Northeastern English city that they had learned their father's plans.

"So, what?" Lauren's voice had been low, derisory, her pink hoodie pulled up and her eyes defiant, though clouded with jet lag. "You're buying a fricken' *island?*"

"Yeah," their father's voice was cool, "you could say that."

4

Once Blamenholm's gate stopped squealing and the stark silence of the castle fell around them, Martha Walker's first instinct was to hide. Within the outer walls, a faint path led in a steep incline through a vast expanse of nodding dock and spiny hood-like nettles. The castle stood at the top of the stubby hill, its slit windows black and lidded, giving it an air of contempt as it glared down at the visitors. Its door was atop a wide flight of stone stairs and curled upward in a tight snarl. The feeling gripping Martha Walker as they began a silent ascent to the castle doors was smallness, vulnerability. The strange treeless flats of the island were unnerving; it reminded her of the silent swoops of the birds of prey they had watched hovering over fields in the early evening, dropping like ghastly bombs.

"Watch your step. Take it slowly on the path."

Saul strode ahead, his army boots squeaking against the damp peat and sodden rock of the jagged path. Like the rest of the islands, the stone beneath them was stacked, uneven, almost impossible to trust—as if a chasm might open suddenly, a black maw sucking greedily at your legs with a freezing tongue.

"Have you noticed the quiet?" Saul stopped abruptly, halfway between the closed gate and the short stone staircase that led to the warped, black wood of the castle door. The Walkers stopped too, unconsciously grouping closer together and staring behind them at the outer wall—which looked strangely distant. Before them, the castle loomed, taller than they had thought it had been. The steady hiss of the sea and the mournful wail of the wind seemed far away behind these walls, as if they had passed into a bubble.

"Everything looks weird, too," Chad said, more to himself than anyone else. "The angles are all... *wrong.*"

Saul looked at him, cocking his head and running a hand through his black curls.

"The castle was built in the early thirteen-hundreds," he said, his voice vague. "There are no surviving records, but it is thought that Scottish prisoners were shipped from their conquered cities to construct this prison."

"Jeez," Martha said, an uncharacteristic frown creasing her forehead.

"Men, women and children were sent to the island with stone hewn from their own burned homes and churches."

Silence again. The Walkers stood, huddled together in the silent rain, staring around at the island which seemed to have become vaster in every sense.

"Like the tombs of ancient Egypt, Blamenholm was built by slaves to appease the gods, constructed from the toil and misery of those it was built to house."

The wind bore the desolate call of a lone seabird overhead. Martha looked upward to see the creature swoop in a vast arc and disappear into the distance. She imagined the lonely tread of Blamenholm's prisoners, their bare feet against the cold jut of stone, their backs bent with pain. A cold finger of ice caressed the back of her neck.

"Did any of them escape?" Chad's voice was a hoarse whisper as he stared up, mesmerized by their dark-clad guide who, like them, stared around at the still, patchy green of the island.

"If you were sent to Blamenholm," Saul said, looking back at Chad's face, glasses streaked with the falling rain and his cheeks red, "you worked or you took your chances in the North Sea."

The faint crash of waves on the rocks, as if in answer, made Chad shiver and he looked from Saul to his father. Martin's face had darkened considerably from the childish excitement he had shown earlier. He stared out to the sea from the virtually undetectable incline of the land behind the castle walls. The grey of the clouds lapped hungrily at the horizon and through them he was sure he saw something, some shape that swayed with the steady rise and fall of the waves. He heard something too, faint, but certainly there: A *creak* of ancient wood, a sound that had hung from the slight salt-stained breeze.

"Well…" Martin's grin was back, but his eyes were determined, almost angry. He clapped his hands together, hard. The sound, which usually echoed around gleaming offices and bounced from the walls of conference centers became a wet-sounding *clop* which was swallowed immediately. "Let's take a last look inside, then."

The others looked at him, puzzled. Martha saw a look on her husband's face she had not seen for many years: the ruthless businessman that had strove tirelessly to break deals, to win negotiations, to push on to victory. This driven force had given them all they had. He had not needed the look for a long time.

"What do you mean, *last*?"

It was Lauren, hood up and hands stuffed inside her sodden waterproof, her eyes aflame. Martha saw in them the same defiance that had once shone from her husband. For a moment, Martha was suddenly afraid of what might happen next. Martin opened his mouth, puffed out his chest, and stared down at his daughter with wide eyes, businessman eyes. Martha moved to her daughter, standing between her and Martin, putting her hands lightly on Lauren's tight shoulder.

"Y'know very well what will happen when Daddy buys the land, honey."

There was laughter in Martha's voice and she kept her eyes on her husband, watching his face as his anger deflated slightly, the grim line of his mouth collapsing and his eyes losing some of their fervor.

Lauren slumped at her mother's touch and an awkward silence fell.

Chad was the one to break it, seemingly oblivious to the strange tension that had passed between them. He stared back up at Saul, who was gazing up at the castle before them.

"Did anyone ever attack the castle, sir?" Chad's voice was bright and hungry for knowledge, a tone of hero-worship becoming evident as he talked to the guide.

Saul broke his stare, shaking his head slightly as if clearing it. His faint laugh was whisked away by the breeze.

"The keep you see before you, my friend," he said, opening his hand to the grey scowl that loomed forward, stretching to see those that stood before it, "has never been breached."

The rain was still falling but had become a fine mist obscuring the horizon. Another cry of a kittiwake echoed from somewhere high in the ramparts.

"There is a story of the only attack on the castle in history." Saul turned and continued toward the castle, the Walkers scurrying in his wake to hear him and not be left behind on the desolate slope. "A band of Border Reivers sailed to Blamenholm. Their plan was to liberate the prisoners and burn the place to the ground…"

"Border Reivers?" Chad looked to his father, who shrugged, his brow creased.

Saul paused to look at the Walkers again, stroking his chin, a curt smile curled across his lips.

"Does the name, 'Elliot' mean anything to you? How about Armstrong? Charlton? Dodd?"

The family looked back, blankly. Then Lauren raised her hand, meekly.

"There was a girl at my school, her surname was 'Dodds.'"

"A-ha." Saul grinned. "A good, Reiver name. Back in the thirteenth century, the very mention of these family names would strike fear into a man like the name of 'Capone' or 'Genovese' did in your country."

"So they were gangsters, these Reivers?" Chad ventured, hopefully.

"Sort of," Saul replied. "They started out as normal families, farmers who just happened to live on the border while Scotland and England went to war."

They had reached the bottom step of the stone stairs that led to the castle doors. In the advancing gloom of the day, the castle did not cast any sort of shadow, but its very presence before them was imposing, with its solid featureless rock, peppered with blackened patches of moss and creeping fingers of lichen.

"Imagine," Saul paused, turning to face the Walkers again, "your crops destroyed, your houses burned, your food taken, your children and livestock killed by every English army heading north, every Scottish army heading south. Every day, another death. Every night you go to sleep and pray you will not be slaughtered where you lay. Eventually, these people decided they had had enough and turned to *reiving*. Not in the name of the Scots or the English, but in their own."

A swell of uncharacteristic anger bubbled inside Martha. What had these people done but tried to scrape out a living during a war? Her mind cast back home to the commercials on the TV, news reports, the tearful shriek of dark-skinned infants muffled by the rattle of automatic weapons, the silent tread of mothers with swollen-bellied kids marching tirelessly from the wreckage of everything they'd ever known.

"What's *reiving*?" Chad asked.

"Fighting back," his mother spat.

"Robbing, looting, stealing, killing." Saul's face was now grim. "English, Scottish, it didn't matter, the Reivers used the cover of darkness to take back what had been taken from them for generations."

The doors before them were thick, blackened wood with long iron hinges that spread from the edges like the pointed nails of some spindly claws. Two black metal rings were fastened into each door, almost blending into the dark wood. They looked like they had not been touched for centuries.

"The Reivers reached these very doors," Saul said as he widened his arms and turned back to the Walkers, pausing for effect, "armed with tall halberds, axes, spears. They easily outnumbered the garrison at the castle…"

The wind began again, and from where they stood on the small hillock, its wails were more audible. Chad's face was intense as he stared up at Saul. When he closed his eyes, he could almost imagine the hot swell of smooth wood in his hands, the righteous fury that coursed through the Reivers as they stared up at this…what? This *horrid* place? No, this… *evil* place where blank-eyed men hung children from hooks and burned fathers feet-first as their bellies were devoured by squealing, starving rodents, the pink foam of gore blossoming on the chests of boys as young as him as they were punctured with black steel…

He shook his head, hard. Where had *that* come from?

Too much of that Resident Eeeeeevil, kiddo! his dad would have said, just like he did when Chad had been reading about some particularly gory episode of history and kept him at the dinner table long after they were finished, asking questions.

"…but that's as far as they got." Saul looked directly upward at the short turret that stood around twenty feet above the doors.

"What happened?" Chad's voice was breathless now, the rest of the family stared at Saul.

"We'll find out when we go inside." Saul's tone was sardonic. He began to fumble again in his pocket, producing a long, black iron key. He scrutinized its curling teeth. "But they never made it back home and Blamenholm castle still stands to this day."

With a deft click, Saul forced the iron key into a small hole above one of the handles.

"One more thing before we enter Blamenholm's keep." Saul turned over his shoulder, looking intently at each of the family in turn.

"Keep to the *edges* of the rooms, do not explore, do not touch, do not go *anywhere* unless I tell you to. Understand?"

The Walkers nodded as one.

With a crunch, Saul undid the lock and heaved the door open. The stale, frozen air of a tomb gusted from the scowling mouth of Blamenholm castle, its expression transformed into a gaping roar of rage.

"Tread carefully…"

"...for the devils of Blamenholm sleep with eyes wide."

"Whist your soft talk, lad!" Walter hissed, cuffing his younger brother around the side of his face.

Robert did not flinch, but was quiet, staring balefully back at Walter, his cheeks tinged blue and eyes wide in the moonlight. One of the shaggy ponies whickered softly somewhere behind them and Walter glared over his shoulder, his eyes fiery above his pale, hollow cheeks. A deep scar curled one side of his mouth into a permanent sneer.

Walter and Robert crouched at the base of the hill amidst a tall bush of stinging nettles through which they had crawled cat-like for around fifty meters, their breaths coming in toothy hisses as the weeds raised white welts on their leathery skin. Both wore light, leather breastplates over shirts of mail, thick, woven scarves around their throats and high, spurred leather boots.

Behind them, the single, disheveled fishing boat that had borne the ten remaining men and their steeds bobbed in the water, clunking hollowly as its prows met the pale rock of Blamenholm Island. Darkness cloaked them as they had sailed from the banks of Beadnell, the horses snorting and stamping their hooves as the men heaved the oars, and the boat rode the stiff waves of the North Sea. The men of the clan huddled together against an outcrop of small boulders, staring across the bleak, flat scape of Blamenholm up at the castle that seemed to lean forward on crooked haunches to leer down at them.

"No fires burn o'er Blamenholm...yet." Walter chuckled. "They've no' seen us." This time he gave his *brother a dig in the ribs with the clump of the remaining fingers on his left hand. Robert only nodded.*

This raid on Blamenholm could have been described as ambitious, but Walter Milburn would only have scoffed. English Reivers of the Middle March clans, Walter and Robert were universally feared throughout the region. The towns that lay on the fringes of both borders had been fortified with watchtowers and wardens, almost exclusively to keep the Milburns' plunder at bay. All livestock was herded safely indoors when night fell. Any sign of riders approaching in the dead of night and the watchtowers that lay on the hills would belch red flame to the sky, followed by swarming clouds of arrows raining down to drive the Reivers back. Wardens now patrolled the roads and the forest paths. And despite the brothers' uncanny ability to navigate the woodland, raids were becoming more and more difficult. A bounty had been placed on both brothers' heads.

"No men, aye," Robert whispered, still staring up at the silent castle.

Walter raised his fist again, snarling at Robert, but then thought better of it and sighed, the fight fizzling from his voice.

"It's our only chance, Rob," he whispered. "Our best men are hanging from trees, their faces food for crows. Your tales of ghosts will send the rest of them into the waves, crying for their mammies! We can't withstand another fight. We need this place."

Robert looked around, breaking his gaze from the castle and stared into his brother's eyes. It took Walter all he had not to look away.

Robert Milburn had been born with a caul, always destined for greatness within the clan, yet it was Walter, born shortly after, who had taken it upon himself to forge his own fearsome reputation. A gangling, aloof boy, Robert had always had a peculiar air about him. He could fight, just as his brother could fight, but he also had the eerie ability to know things before they happened. As they grew older, it had been Robert who had known about ambushes by the wardens, seen the outcomes of their battles in his dreams. It was this ability that had raised their clan to greatness in the borderlands. With Walter's brawn and Robert's clairvoyance, they had carved the name of Milburn into the landscape with bloodied steel.

"You're right." Robert nodded. "Just promise me one thing."

"What?"

"We will not stay here."

The wind began to pick up, whistling through the steel flaps of the brothers' helmets.

"Why, Robert?" Walter was speaking through his teeth, his fury returning. "It is only slaves and old men who guard these walls. We can take this place, we can regroup, and Blamenholm can be ours!"

Robert turned back to the castle, sighing softly, his breath whistling with the wind.

"Do you not think others have thought the same, brother?" His voice was pained, almost tearful. "It is not men who guard the walls of Blamenholm, but death. The Norsemen awoke something here long ago. Something they could not control. Something that will not rest."

Walter felt a chill at his brother's words. He stared up at the lonely castle on the hill, silhouetted in a ghastly shadow by the light of the moon. Robert carried on, his face vacant, eyes following Walter's gaze.

"This was the place they danced for days around their pyres of dead holy-men. Where men turned to *wolves in the presence of their one-eyed war-God...there's more than men that walk that place, brother."*

Eventually, his voice resigned, Walter spoke.

"We'll plunder the innards of the place for everything it is worth. We'll kill beasts for food and leave the dead. Then when first light rises over the Farnes, we'll leave." Walter looked at Robert, waiting for his approval.

After a few moments, Robert nodded. "Gather the men. Seven longbows guard the wall. Let's make this quick."

6

It was difficult to anticipate what lay behind the scowling, gnarled exterior of Blamenholm castle; the thick grey of its walls, lashed for years by the sting of sea fret gave no clue. One would almost be forgiven for imagining the deep chestnut of polished wood and the wine-blushed scarlet of carpets, the plush Victoriana that graced the innards of the majority of England's ancient fortresses. There was something about Blamenholm, however, that did not smack of such things. Even its proximity to the freezing rage of the North Sea did not conjure the proud bows and whipping crack of sails, preserved creatures from the depths of the oceans, glazed glass for eyes, staring from faded mounts on stone walls. In fact, the hollow emptiness that greeted the Walkers as Saul heaved wide the door was the last thing any of them had expected.

The family moved closer together as they stepped through the threshold of Blamenholm's walls, their arms touching slightly as the drop in temperature rose raw gooseflesh on their tanned, American skin. Light fell lamely inside from the few slits of windows high inside, casting a sickly, blue pallor on the stony stillness of the castle's interior. They stared up and around at the ceiling that swept upward in a sharp concave, its broad summit engulfed in blackness. At each corner, there were several more black spots that coiled upward into the dark. Vast cobwebs trickled from every corner, wispy at their edges but intricate and thick as carpet the further they rose, their occupants invisible and still. There appeared to be only this bare hall, its floor uneven and its corners dark. The floor on which they stood was disconcertingly uneven, as if it had been hacked straight from some curved hollow.

"Wow," Chad breathed, his voice muffled by the strange curvature of the ceiling.

Saul closed the outer door with a creaking thud before taking a few purposeful steps in front of them, producing a large flashlight from somewhere inside his coat. Instead of illuminating the black hollows of this strange place, he shone the light on the floor a few feet in front of the Walkers.

"Come forward please, and stay close."

His voice was calm but firm. The twinkle that had skipped in his eyes as he had described the sieges and battles that had been fought outside its walls had been extinguished by the oppressive chill of Blamenholm's interior. The Walkers, standing in the yellow pool of light and looking at him with wide eyes, agreed simultaneously

"You're right to feel strange," he began, then stopped, his mouth open, his eyes darting for a millisecond to the corners of the hall and all around, as if waiting for something.

There was total silence, and the Walkers unknowingly began shifting closer to each other. Even the screech of the wind from outside had been silenced by the odd, airlock effect of the closed door. Saul shook his head and continued.

"The inside of the castle was designed for one specific purpose and one alone." He pointed at Chad, the only member of the Walker family who was not looking at Saul but staring around at the odd curves of the ceiling. "How do you feel right now, eh?"

Chad turned bright eyes back to Saul.

"I'm like... kinda... confused..." he said, picking his words carefully.

Lauren spoke too, now, but with a slight tone of derision in her voice.

"It's *nasty*… you can't see around anything. It's like the inside of a…"

"Shell." Both Walkers spoke in unison. Saul smiled wryly at this and dropped his voice.

"Exactly," he said, shining his torch briefly at one of the hall's dark corners which seemed to curl upward into more darkness and a thick plateau of cobwebs.

"We think that Blamenholm was built this way on purpose. The whole point of the place was to make the people who were imprisoned here feel *nasty*, to make them…"

Saul stopped again, and this time the silence was punctuated by a faint rumbling from somewhere either behind or in front of them, like the rattle of a pipe. Saul shook his head again and continued, his voice picking up speed.

"The only windows are high up, to see *out* of. There was no need for windows down here—" Saul glanced up, shining the torch briefly again at the narrow slits high in the walls.

"The Reivers decided they would sail out to Blamenholm to claim the castle, they made sure, first of all, that their boats were not destroyed by the rocks. They made it past the archers at the outer walls and fought their way into the keep, standing where we are now, looking at what *appears* to be an empty hallway and nothing else, right?"

The Walkers nodded and Saul motioned them to move backward. He shone the flashlight fleetingly at the still stone of one of the walls and followed their steps. When the family was as close as they could be to the left hand wall of the great hall, a few inches from touching the stone itself, Saul regained the thread of his explanation.

"The door to the keep had been left open." His voice took on a grave quality, eerie the way it did not echo in the odd darkness of the castle. "And the raiders stood where you were just stood, staring around…unsure of where to go…"

This time Saul paused for a second, glancing around. There was another pipe-like clatter from somewhere else in the darkness and Lauren's teeth had begun to chatter in the still cold. To her the castle was not quiet, no, the castle was *loud*.

She was finding it difficult to keep track of Saul's words, alongside the eerie rushing sound that no one else seemed to be able to hear, all around the spiraling ceilings and passageways of the castle, things were moving. The flicker of shadows and the skitter of spider legs on long-cold stone. There seemed to be invisible eyes everywhere, those gross bulbous, insect eyes that in no way had a soul, eyes that had not looked on people for hundreds of years. They were hungry, those eyes, and they could see every twitch of her head, every movement of her eye. She could feel panic starting to descend, a fight-or-flight impulse that was racing up and down her arms and it was all she could do not to whip around to face the entrance they had come in, because it would not be there, there would just be wall and if she looked back, they would all be gone and it would just be her and the rush of quiet that would reach up with its hand that stank of sea and—

"That's when the garrison at Blamenholm released their trap."

This time Saul pointed the torch directly at the ceiling, shining it back and forth, illuminating what hung high in the concave darkness above them. The

Walkers gave a collective gasp. Lauren grasped hold of her mother's arm in a pretty childish way but right now she did not give *a flying fuck, no siree.*

Hanging on cobweb-encrusted black chains were what appeared to be a series of portcullis style gates that were concealed snugly in the gloom of the ceiling's curve. They were made of thick, dark metal with cruel, uneven spikes on their lower halves and they hung there, motionless from their chains.

"Jesus," Martin Walker whispered.

"The weight of them alone would break your bones." Saul kept the light on the ghastly prongs that hung like rows of uneven, shark-like teeth in the cobwebs high above them. "If you were lucky, it would pierce your skull or your throat and you would die quickly."

"And if you weren't?" Chad's boyish fascination with such instruments of torture was audible in his tone as he gazed up at the sharpened metal above them.

"They would not wait for you to pull your arm or leg free." Saul moved his flashlight further and further back, making it clear that the whole of the ceiling was filled with row after row of iron spines. "They would pull them up again, fast and they would watch as you fell from however high you got."

He stamped his foot, making a *thunk* sound that did not reverberate but sent a collective shiver through the Walkers.

"Hence the stone floor."

Saul dipped the light to the ground, letting the perpetual darkness swallow the ceiling again.

There were a few moments of eerie silence in the black belly of Blamenholm castle as the five people stared around. There was more thudding from somewhere above them as what sounded like another pipe began clearing itself.

"I've never heard of *anything* like this in my life…" Martin Walker whispered, his eyes pale and wide in the weak light.

Saul nodded, his eyes downcast.

"The Sages have never allowed historians or archaeologists to conduct research on Blamenholm," he said, gravely. "When they inherited the place, they burned all records, every document, everything that's known as *fact* about what went on here has been passed on by word alone."

"But why—" Martin began but Saul cut him off.

"And that's how they would like it to stay."

His tone was so abrupt that Martin faltered and stopped. There was another few seconds of silence until Chad piped up.

"Sir…" his voice carried a sudden weight, a heavy respect. "Does the castle have a *dungeon*?"

As Chad spoke this final word, a few things happened. First something flickered across Saul's face, gone so quick a blink would have missed it. For a millisecond his expression, which had been neutral all the way through the tour of the place, filled with a ghost-like horror. Second, an audible creak came from the darkness above them, the screech of ancient metal. Martha Walker let out a shriek and pulled her children close against her, backing into the wall. The thudding from the pipe grew in intensity almost to the point where one might believe that there was no way this ancient place contained any pipes whatsoever and that someone—some*thing*—was in fact jumping up and down in a psychotic jig on one of the upper floors.

"Stay close," Saul muttered, moving to the wall with the Walkers and shining his flashlight back up at the ceiling. Nothing moved. The diabolical trap was still. He cleared his throat and regained his dour composure.

"Blamenholm castle was built for one reason, to contain." He began walking, slowly back to the closed entrance door. "Once you were inside the dungeon, if you even made it there, you did not get out."

The Walkers, now holding tight to each others' hands, followed him closely. Their breath fogged gently in the frozen air.

"The remains of those that were condemned to Blamenholm still lie in manacles untouched in the deep below the castle, the place where day and night don't differ."

This last line sent a shiver across Chad's forearms, and he was glad of the thick fleece that hid them from view.

Yeah kiddo, dungeons were *cool*, when we're sitting in Ms. Kirsh's history class with Jake and Eddie, looking through the textbook and drawing the rack and the gibbet in our books. Dungeons were *cool* then, when the sun's hot outside and the smell of hotdogs from the cafeteria is just trickle under the door and making stomachs rumble. Pretty cool huh? Pretty neat? *Too much Resident Eeeeeevil.*

Imagining a place darker and more frightening than here in this hateful place made Chad feel sick and he wanted to shout to his dad, he wanted to holler in his face, *Dad! We're not going down there, okay? Just in case, just in case you were thinking I'd think a dungeon would be pretty cool right now, it wouldn't, okay? It really would not be cool AT ALL.*

They reached the door and Saul stopped, rolling up his sleeve and shining the flashlight upon the ragged pink of a cruel scar that twisted around his wrist and carried up along his forearm.

Dad! You're not going to let him open that door, OKAY? We have NO IDEA what is going to come crawling the hell out of there!

"I have only ventured down there once in my life," he said, voice almost a whisper, face wincing at the memory. "To access the dungeon, you must walk down one hundred uneven stairs, single file, in pitch darkness. The stairwell is narrow and its ceiling is low. For my safety as well as yours, we will not venture there today."

Saul heaved at the keep door, the dim light from outside now a pale window in the darkness.

As the Walkers and Saul made their way from the glare of Blamenholm castle, to the boat that was rocking and thudding against the blunt stone of the island, Martin Walker was deep in thought; the voice inside his head was resigned.

As soon as all the legal bullshit is over, he was going to rip this foul place up by its roots, and bury the misery of Blamenholm deep in the ocean where it belongs. *This island would see the sun once more... he swore it.*

7

Despite the morning's rain, the afternoon had opened into clear skies that beamed down onto the pale yellow farmland of the Northumbrian countryside. The air was still, save for the lazy hum of flies and the flashes of color from the occasional wagtails that flitted from hedgerow to hedgerow. As evening fell, the burr of woodpigeons began to count the fading of the daylight. Little traffic traversed the sleek tarmac of the long, Roman roads that headed for the horizon and the calm blue of the North Sea perched on the periphery of the land, the fuzzy brown of the Farne Islands with the white pillars of their light houses just visible in the fading light.

A few miles inland from the spectacular coastline, the damp green and brown of the moorlands sloped upward to form the toes of the Cheviot Hills. These crags and knolls formed the heather-clad black land where slim bridleways snaked lazily through the grasses and stone tracks zigzagged to meet the rush of the water from the burns that swirled from the hills into the River Till.

It was on one of these tributaries of the Till, known as Wooler Water, where the five star converted mill-to-holiday-cottage stood. Its wheel hung from one great wall that ran beside the river, a shining, black archaism, still, despite the buffering of the water. The white-barked birch trees grew around the mill in clumps, pale fingers topped with sagging green leaves and the occasional burst of whites and reds from the bushy hawthorns of the surrounding forest. From the outside, the mill's gray walls gave it an air of ancient authenticity. Only the state of the art double glazing and entrance door, along with the twin black cars parked outside, let on that the cottage existed in the present. A winding, single lane track led from the mill, through the forest and out for six miles to the nearest village. Save for the rush of the river and the rustlings from the trees as night creatures awoke and the birds began their prissy roosting in the branches, there was quiet in the still air.

On the top floor of the converted mill, Martha and Martin Walker sat in a wide, king-sized bed, both wearing soft bathrobes. Neither concentrated on the high definition television screen that flickered on the wall at the bed's foot. The carpet of their bedroom was thick and soft, an en suite bathroom gleamed with clean silver pipes and switches and a faint smell of potpourri drifted from the dark wood of their dressing table. The ceiling was interlaced with polished wooden beams that had been here since the mill was built. They had pulled the blind halfway down the large window, despite there not being any civilized populace for a few square miles, nor any chance of anyone being able to see in. They were suburban people and set in their ways.

Martin had a MacBook propped on his lap and was scrolling through a number of PDF files, muttering to himself and writing notes on a pad of paper with his right hand. His iPhone lay beside him on the bed, silenced at his wife's request. He was still quietly frustrated at Saul's absolute refusal to let any of them take photographs inside the castle itself. Instead, Saul had emailed Martin a folder of scanned photographs of the castle's interior, taken sometime in the early 1990s. There was little change to what they had seen themselves: the shell-like curvature of the corners and the black void of ceiling that hid the despicable metal spikes remained as they were. Martin had received several interior designs from his architects for the development of Blamenholm into a Gateway resort. These plans had to be scrutinized and approved for a development meeting in the morning. As usual, Martin insisted on going over every detail with a fine toothcomb. His scrupulous notes as testament to this.

Martha was wearing her glasses and was turning the virtual pages of the latest Jo Nesbø novel on her Kindle Fire (7-inch HD of course, only the best for you, kiddo). A cup of green tea that had long gone cold balanced precariously on the duvet beside her left elbow. Both of them were unused to this level of tranquility. They were acclimatized to the steady roar of traffic or the whirr of air conditioning back home. The thick, double-glazed windows blocked the grumble of Wooler Water entirely, and it had only been when Martin had flicked on the television and turned down the volume to a low burble that they had both been able to relax.

The sound that broke the calm of the evening sent Martha's Kindle almost flying from her hands, and Martin gave a small cry, his computer toppling backward onto his knees. The forgotten cup of tea shuddered as they both jumped, miraculously managing to keep hold of its contents. It was a bang, a single, thick sound as if somewhere in the cottage, a door had been kicked rather than slammed shut.

Martin and Martha looked at each other with matching expressions of surprise and confusion.

"The hell was that?" Martin swung his feet from the bed, leaving his computer lying screen up before him. It was not immediately clear where the sound had come from, and the absolute silence in its wake was disconcerting. It was certainly not their door, there was no obvious reverberation in the room and there were no other doors on the top floor of the old mill. Both Walkers stared around, puzzled. The sound had been slightly muffled but too clear to have come from downstairs.

"The kids…" Martha's tone was one of pale irritation, rather than panic.

Chad and Lauren had their own en suite bathrooms on the floor below them, and below that was the wide, white kitchen that led into the sitting room with three long, leather sofas, open fireplace and thick rugs. The lower level of the cottage had been converted into a game room of sorts, carpeted in an inviting aquamarine blue with a velvet snooker table, dartboard and iPod docking station connected to large speakers in the wall. The Walker children had not shown the slightest interest in these things, preferring to keep their own company in their rooms. Arguments between the two were rare. They hadn't entirely outgrown bickering with each other; their occasional spats were accompanied by slamming doors, petulant wails, and stomping feet.

"I'll go check." Martin was irritated now, pulling his bathrobe around him and tightening the cord, he slipped his feet into a complimentary pair of cotton slippers and walked around the huge bed to the door.

"I'll come too."

The noise had unnerved Martha slightly. She was not superstitious (she was barely religious), but she knew that whatever was going on, she did not want to be left alone in the bedroom.

The staircase leading to the lower floor was in darkness. Martin flicked the light switch, but no illumination was forthcoming.

"Damn fuses…"

They descended the narrow staircase in the dark, their toes in the thick carpet making no sound. The floorboards did not creak in this sort of accommodation. The fuses, however, were not as high of quality. Reaching the first floor of the mill, Martha and Martin looked down the long corridor: one black doorway at the end that led down to the kitchen and living room, two other doors on either side. The children's' bedrooms.

Despite the darkness of the staircase, the lights in the first floor corridor were working. Two energy saving bulbs high in the ceiling that flickered on with initial dimness. The door to Lauren's room was ajar and yellow lamplight was spilling from inside. Knocking gently, Martin opened the door and poked his head inside. His daughter lay beneath the covers, her own MacBook on her lap, headphones on and the bright colors of some film lighting up her cheeks. Martha made as if to speak, but Martin shook his head and motioned them both back out of the room. Lauren did not notice Martin and Martha as they backed out, closing the door behind them.

Chad's room was on the opposite side of the dark corridor. The oak paneled door was shut tight and Martin rapped gently with his knuckles. A few seconds went by until they heard a murmur of consent.

Pushing Chad's door open, both Martin and Martha instantly reacted to the cold rush of air that greeted them. The bedroom was similar to their own: large with a plush bed, large flat screen television and en suite bathroom. The only difference in Chad's room was that there was an open fireplace, with a large, jutting chimney in the wall. Chad had been told explicitly not to make use of it by his father. If he got too cold, there were several radiators and a heated towel rail he could turn on. The weather had been fine in the afternoon, however, and none of the family had felt the need for the cottage's central heating.

The sudden cold in Chad's room was quite a shock. Martin stepped a few feet inside, shivering slightly, and looked to his son stretched out on the bed, lying horizontal, hands splayed at his sides. He had the look of someone who'd just been dropped from a great height and did not have the courage to move yet. His room was in darkness, save for the blue hue of evening light from the window. There were no lights on, no illuminated phone screen in his hand, his Xbox was not even plugged in. It just lay redundant in the corner, a cold black square. Chad, however *was* awake, he looked up lazily at his parents who looked at each other, confused.

"Chad, honey," his mother said, gently, "it's freezing in here."

Chad looked up at Martha. He had taken off his glasses and his eyes were bright in the dimness of the room. For a few seconds, he did not do nor say anything, and Martha was filled with a sudden, irrational terror. They stood for what felt like longer than a few seconds in the dark of Chad's room, staring down at their son. He just stared back at them, his face blank.

"It's colder on this side of the house, son," Martin broke the strange silence, making Martha jump slightly. She wondered what was wrong with her tonight.

Ignoring his son's strange, passive silence, he strode over to the window that was halfway open, clearly the source of the freezing air. As he closed it, he looked out onto the motionless waterwheel that hung from the cottage. The forest was dark and still around them.

"Keep this shut, you hear?"

Martin looked down at Chad, whose gaze seemed to break from the strange fogginess that it held moments earlier.

"Sorry, Dad," his voice was meek, apologetic.

"Hey, it's okay, son!" A smile had come back into Martin's tone. He pulled the window shut and clicked on the bedside lamp, bathing the room in a calm glow. Chad's eyes squinted slightly. He had obviously been lying for a long time in the semi-darkness listening to the chatter of the river against the mill wheel.

"Thinking, huh?" he said, ruffling Chad's thin crop of blonde hair.

"I guess."

Martha hovered in the doorway. She did not feel quite right. Always a woman to trust her instinct, something inside her, some strange impulse, was nudging at her brain.

"I'm gonna go check on Lauren again, okay? Just gonna ask if she heard…" she said, almost in a whisper before drifting backward and out into the dark of the corridor.

Martin nodded at her, still smiling.

"Heard what, Dad?"

Chad straightened from his collapsed position.

"You and your sister been fighting, son?" Martin said, his humor still good.

Chad looked confused.

"Nah," he said, shaking his head and reaching for his glasses. Martin placed them in his hand. "I was just thinking about the castle, Dad, it's so *cool*."

Martin smiled down at his son and swung his legs up on the bed.

"Did you know," Chad's voice was strained with sudden enthusiasm, "they used to *impale* people on the walls?"

"Gruesome stuff." Martin nodded. "It was pretty harsh back then, you know?"

"Yeah!" Chad grinned back. "Saul said there was a bad man who lived there. He used to keep the children in cages and feed them, to get them fat, like in that kids' story... then he used to cook them!"

Martin shook his head, his grin widening.

"Come on now, son," he said, "that was all a long, long time ago, and you know what I think?"

"What?"

"I think Saul made most of it up. He got paid a lot of money to show us round today."

Chad's eagerness dimmed, his mouth turned down into an almost comical expression of anger.

"Uh-*uhh*," he protested. "Saul said it was true!"

"Enough now." Martin stood up, shaking his head again. "Less of that talk. You'll give yourself bad dreams."

"No way!" Chad was scornful at this suggestion. "He also—"

"Chad," Martin cut him off, changing the subject. "Why were you lying here with the lights off and the window open when we came in?"

"Oh," Chad said, "I heard something outside, running around in the yard. I looked out, but it stopped, so I thought if I lay still, I might hear it again."

"Hear what?" Martin looked to the window, where the dark branches of trees were nodding slightly in the breeze.

"Do they have wolves in England, Dad?"

"I don't think so, not anymore."

"Oh."

Quiet again for a second or two, Chad wriggled his feet underneath the duvet and yawned.

"We're in a forest, son." Martin felt tired himself, and the bang seemed a long time ago now. It had clearly been no work of either of the children. "There's a lot of wildlife, it was probably a fox or a deer or something."

Martin got to his feet, where he had sat still left an indent in the thick memory foam of the bed. He took two steps over to the door and turned the handle.

"Uh-*uh*," Chad chimed again, his voice thick with weariness. "It was a wolf."

Faint laughter drifted from Lauren's room along the corridor. Martin heard Martha's feet ascending the stairs back to their bedroom.

"Get some sleep, son." Martin smiled, waving goodnight to Chad, whose eyes were already closed.

"Night, Dad," Chad whispered.

Martin shut Chad's bedroom door slowly and made his way back upstairs. If he had looked around, he would have seen the light in Chad's room, which spilled under the door, clicking gently off.

8

"Where the hell is the goddamned thing?" Martin stifled his exclamation. What would have been a full throated roar of sheer frustration became a wavering screech of fury that whistled from behind his teeth.

The innocent blue of the morning shone jauntily through the window, lighting what had, the night before, been the serene order of Martha and Martin's bedroom. Now, however, the room appeared like it had been ripped apart by a small whirlwind. Drawers hung from their wooden chests. Both wardrobe doors stood wide, belching expensive cotton shirts onto the bedspread that had been hurled onto the floor. Martin stood atop the destruction, twin spots of rage red on his cheeks. He was dressed in only his pajama bottoms, small beads of sweat on the silky line of hair that expanded from his stomach and bushed on his chest. His usually calm but determined countenance was creased with fury and his hair stood in disheveled clumps where he had run both hands through it in desperation.

"I'm going downstairs," Martha said, carefully making her way to the bedroom door.

Martha had seen these rages before. Thankfully they were short lived and dissipated instantly if Martin found the thing he had lost. Her husband's meticulous organization usually prevented this sort of occurrence. In fact, she suspected that one of the reasons that Martin was so organized was that deep down he was slightly ashamed of his almost child-like temper tantrums when he lost something. Organization prevented it ever happening. Years ago, Martha had tried to placate him but soon grew to learn that her offers and suggestions of where things had been left were always met with a grim silence, a frustrated sigh or were simply ignored. By now, Martha knew to leave well alone and let the whirlwind burn itself out.

As Martha descended the sleek staircases to the ground floor of the old mill and the sounds of Martin stamping around the bedroom, wrenching drawers in and out and slamming the wardrobe doors grew fainter, Martha pondered the source of her husband's rage: the iPhone that had been charging on his bedside table which, charger included, had not been present when their digital radio awoke them this morning.

On the ground floor of the mill, the kitchen was empty. Chad and Lauren were still in their rooms. She could hear the faint hiss of the shower on Lauren's side of the first floor, behind it roared the strange quiet of this part of the world. With a slightly tenuous step, Martha padded into the kitchen and busied herself with coffee, watching through the window at the sight of a plump wood pigeon and a goldfinch, simultaneously descending onto the wide bird table from one of the tall trees that surrounded the mill. She clanked the carafe probably louder than she should have and hummed to herself. At home, the large television screen which she had begged Martin not to install in the kitchen for *chrissakes*—who watches TV in the kitchen?—would have burbled CNN or Fox News to cover the roar of the trucks and cars that rattled along the freeway, the sight of which was hidden by hedges but permeated every waking moment with its drone.

In this place, Martha could really hear things, almost as if she had awakened from some extended jet lag. The wind purred and rattled through the leaves of the trees and the sea spoke in contented, regular hisses from the horizon.

Strangely, she had not heard the bang that had awoken her husband the previous night. When Martin had sat bolt upright in bed, Martha had already been awake for a while, listening to the giggles and footsteps of the children who were charging up and down the corridor of the floor below. Of course when she and Martin had gone down to check, Chad and Lauren had run back to their bedrooms, feigning peace. The puzzling thing was that when Martha had gone to see Lauren, unimpressed with Chad lying on his bed in the dark, pretending he hadn't been doing anything, Lauren had denied everything. It was hard for Martha to press her daughter, who seemed as puzzled as she, claiming she had been simply lying in bed and watching DVDs on her MacBook all evening. "Oh my *God*, Mom! What are you talking about?" had been her response when pushed for an explanation as to why she and Chad had been running about half the night. Martha was irked by her daughter's tetchy response. Lately they had been getting on like a mother and daughter *should*; they shared safe little jokes and she had taken to asking Lauren how her own hair looked, turning away to bite her bottom lip, the mocking tone of her own mother echoing from somewhere long buried.

Good ol' boy material, my girl… fit for bringin' up babies in a barn…

Martha had stayed awake for several hours, feeling the ancient reverberations of fury that had punctured the affection she felt for her own mother as it sagged into resentment, concluding in a sodden pool of mutual, silent hate. She lay listening to the faint crash of the sea that was strangely audible through the cottage's double glazing, as was a lonely *creak* of what sounded like sails.

There was a sound at the kitchen doorway. Martha turned from the birds that were feasting hungrily on two pale suet blocks to see her daughter. Lauren was dressed in a too-big gray hoodie and pajama bottoms, she wore no makeup, and her hair was scraped into a rough ponytail. She had an expression of confusion on her sleep-creased face and was holding something in her hands. Martha, about to offer her daughter a cup of coffee balked when she realized that winking gently in Lauren's hands was Martin's iPhone and charger.

"Lauren?" Martha walked toward her daughter, her head cocked.

"Before you ask…" Lauren's voice was thick with sleep and spiky with confused irritation, "I have no idea what it was doing in my room, okay?"

"But wha—?" Martha reached out her hands and was taken aback as Lauren slammed the phone into them.

"I said I don't *know*, okay?" she snapped, turning on her heel and storming back through the kitchen.

Outrage flashed swiftly through Martha. Lauren was occasionally a little moody, but this was unprovoked defiance. The voice that had leaped like a bark from her daughter's mouth was not Lauren, not in a million years. It was her own. Martha *Swan* from oh so long ago, Martha *good ol' boy material* Swan who had taken jibe after jibe and slight after slight until it was time to tell her sweet ol' mamma where she could stick her *pseudo-righteousness-bullshit,* and oh how good it had felt for those words to come rolling off her tongue in a scream and the silence that echoed deafeningly in her ears when she'd closed that door for the last time and never gone back.

But it was happening, it was happening again and this time it was not Martha, it was Lauren. Dear God, had she become…

"Wait a minute, young lady!" Martha called, her voice suddenly loud, booming from somewhere deep in her stomach. This time her voice was not her own, but Momma's. To her shock and burning shame, it came spiraling off her tongue in that drawl that Momma had spent so much time trying to hide, but when her emotions got the better of her, when her own *goddamn daughter wanted to go wasting her time in the backs of boys' cars instead of doing her goddamn studies and end up in bed with some hick hogger, which is what I did, my girl and is where y'all will end up if you have your way!*

"You just get your sorry ass back here where I can see you! Don't you DARE walk out that door!"

Lauren looked round, more in surprise than anything else and that's when the carafe of freshly brewed coffee went flying from its warming plate on the counter, shattering on the kitchen floor, splinters of glass and rich-smelling brown liquid exploding across the pale linoleum.

Martha and Lauren both screamed in unison, Martha jumping instinctively away from the insipid chestnut puddle that rolled hungrily toward her feet. They both took several steps backward, out of the open-plan kitchen and onto the carpet of the sitting room, staring back into the still kitchen, the only sound the pop and hiss from the empty plate of the coffee machine.

"Mom?" Lauren's voice, after a few seconds of shocked silence, contained none of the petulance from before. In fact, she had regained that odd little-girl tone she had adopted in the car the previous night.

"Don't worry honey," Martha said, her voice remarkably level, "I'll get that. Must have pulled the wire or something…"

Good one, kiddo, the only wire on the damn thing was still hopped around the back and plugged into the wall. Even if she had pulled it, it would have taken *effort* to get the thing to smash like that, but Jesus Christ it was good to feel Lauren's hand in her own now, where it belonged. Yes, because when she heard that voice rising out of her like some long-dead ghost, green with slime from some stagnant pool of her brain, she could have said anything, something that she would not be able to take back. It was too close. When it came down to it, it didn't matter what had happened to the coffee pot, it mattered that Lauren was still hers.

With trembling hands, Martha Walker plucked a fresh tea towel from a hook on the side of the counter and knelt down, sweeping the glass and puddle of lukewarm coffee together with two hands.

"Give me a hand, then." Her voice was quiet, but firm.

Without a word of protest, Lauren joined her mother on the kitchen floor.

9

With his iPhone recovered and with no time for questions or explanations, Martin Walker left for his meeting. The car's wheels crunched on the gravel as he drove from the mill cottage, where his wife and children sat around the dining table munching cereal and sipping orange juice. The incident with the coffee had nearly been forgotten; neither of them said it, but both Martha and Lauren were finding it difficult recalling exactly what had happened not even an hour ago. Both resigned themselves to the fact that there had been a simple accident and the glass carafe had smashed. That made the most sense. That was easiest.

Today, Martha and the children were off to visit the castle and gardens at Alnwick, a small market town an hour or so south from the cottage. Lauren was particularly excited about the place. Alnwick castle provided many a backdrop and location for the *Harry Potter* movies, the books of which she still secretly loved. There were plenty of medieval jousting and battle displays that would satisfy Chad's boyish fascination with warfare and the macabre. Martha was already blown away with the majesty of the North Eastern English countryside, the viridian hills that dotted with white blossoms of sheep and the crooked forests were a million miles from the flat fields of her hometown. She perused the website over breakfast for the castle garden. It showed neat hedgerows and sheathes of ornamental flowers growing around a tumbling cascade water feature of freshly sand-blasted stone. It was a thousand miles from the crooked gray stone of Blamenholm.

Martin's abrupt change of mood after his phone had been discovered was not unexpected. He had kissed his wife full on the lips, his face blushing like a teenage boy as he had left. Lauren seemed to have forgotten the sulk in which she had awoken and was tucking into one of the juicy Craster kippers she had taken to in the few days they had been here. Chad held his nose.

"That stinks!" Chad chided, looking at his sister's plate, but Lauren only grinned, cocking her head to one side.

"Low in fat, high in protein and omega-3, not to mention pretty darn tasty!" she said, her eyes playful.

Martha looked up from her laptop, laughing.

"You ever consider going into infomercials, honey?"

"What's omega?" Chad asked, through a mouthful of cereal.

"Brain food, smarty pants. You should try it sometime," his sister said, winking at her mother.

Lauren dug another forkful of flesh from the smoked fish on her plate and laughed. The sudden change of mood had affected everyone, and the mood around the breakfast table was upbeat.

Martha sighed and lifted herself from the table. "Can you kids put all your things in the dishwasher while I go get ready?"

They needed to set off soon. Martha was dressed but needed to fix her hair and apply a light layer of Estee Lauder, not to obscure, it was too late in life for that, but simply lift the wrinkles that were growing with the passing years. She also knew that she would have to straighten up in the bedroom; Martin's brief rage had scattered most of their clothes from the drawers and wardrobe as he had searched in vain for his phone.

She shivered slightly, remembering his blazing blue eyes, the snarl curled on his face as he stomped around the bedroom. She'd only seen him like that before once or twice and, thank Christ, not in front of the kids. Always over something dumb: a missing sock or shoe, the Internet conking out with no reasonable explanation. Best thing to do was to leave him to it, let the fury burn itself out because there was sure as hell no reasoning with him when he was like that. She often wondered if it was this slightly unhinged demeanor when something wasn't going exactly his own way that made the difference at work.

He was in the cut and thrust of the business world after all. Maybe being slightly unhinged sometimes was an asset?

With noises of assent from the children, Martha made her way up the two flights of stairs toward the top floor of the cottage. Another strange, *tight* feeling, the same tense air as this morning before Martin had left. It felt very quiet and very cold up here, despite the warmth and joviality of the breakfast table. Stopping for a moment on the short landing of the first floor, she listened for the familiar clinks and clanks of the dishwasher being loaded and the high voices as the children bantered back and forth. There was nothing. It was as if the staircase was a vacuum. Martha suddenly felt very alone, a peculiar sensation that tugged at her heartstrings and raised her hackles gently. For some reason, she did not want to look down the long corridor toward Lauren and Chad's bedrooms. In fact, she turned her head purposefully away and hurried past that doorway. Nope, she thought, I ain't even going there sweetheart. It was like there was something there something for her to see and the horrible thought that brought her out in gooseflesh on a summer's afternoon, the terrible notion that swam from nowhere into her mind was that she'd see the face of Uncle Karl. But this time it *would* be a skull. He'd be turned around in his faded jeans and blue-checked shirt and he'd gurgle through a grinning lipless mouth, "Y'all okay back there, ladies?"

She ran up the stairs, lips tight against a scream that spring-boarded itself from her tongue. That's when another sound stopped her dead, halfway up the second flight of stairs. It was the familiar, cushioned thump of something landing on a carpeted floor. For some reason though, this sounded *timed*, it sounded somehow menacing. The hair on Martha's arms and neck sprung taut and swift terror spilled into her stomach. The noise had come from the children's corridor, as if it had read her thoughts.

"I won't!" Martha hissed out loud, hurrying up the second flight of stairs, adrenaline now hurtling though her as she grasped the door handle of her and Martin's bedroom, heart pounding and breath rasping in the back of her throat.

The door swung open with a faint whisper of the polished wood against thick carpet. Martha Walker made to step forward but let out a scream. She clapped her hands to her mouth to suppress it but was unsuccessful. Her eyes wide, she stared around at the bedroom, suppressing another wavering shriek at the sight that met her eyes.

It was immaculate.

The chaos from Martin's ransacking of the room for his phone had been cleared away. Not just cleared away either. The room looked like it had the day they arrived: the sheets of the bed pulled taut, pillows fluffed up and the surfaces gleaming. Was that the lingering odor of wood polish in the air?

An old smell brought another sudden onset of memory careening into her brain. It was the mournful smell of stillness, the quiet of the big house where her mother had died all those years ago. The smell of the polish brought back the empty acceptance that had filled her, heavy as lead the day they had returned from the sparse funeral to collect her few possessions, never to return. That house had felt more full of her mother's quiet fury than it ever had when she was alive. Her disapproval shone from every room, not just a spiteful emanation from the creaking rocker before the empty, black fireplace in the front room.

Lowering her hands gently, Martha stood in the bedroom doorway, staring around in wonder, reeling from the memories that had filled her so uncharacteristically. She did not dare to take a step forward, even the carpet looked like it had been cleaned, every strand standing on end. Staring across the room's shining stillness, Martha could see the blind on the window had been opened fully and the trees that surrounded the mill stood still, casting green-infused sunlight in pools on the bed. The whole scene was idyllic, like some photograph from a brochure. Even their possessions had been tidied away: toiletries lined up in order of size on the chest of drawers, towels hung in neat, blue squares in the gleaming bathroom.

With a trembling hand, Martha reached for the handle of the door that she had let swing inward. She would not look down, her eyes were fixed forward because that was what normal folks did, normal folks did not get the jitters in luxury accommodation for the love of God! The polished surfaces glared back, patient, glimmering like the eyes of a cat. Martha raised her hand, as if feeling her way forward. As the bare skin of her hand passed beyond the gloss-coated paint of the doorframe, she felt her fingers dip into the wall of freezing air. The sunlight that sat in golden pools on the bed was not the frost-tinged sunlight of a bleak autumn afternoon back home, but the full-blooded beam of a summer's day. The window was tightly closed and the rest of the house was comfortably warm. Martha withdrew her hand with a gasp, clutching the tips of her fingers in her opposite palm.

"Mom!"

Jesus, Chad. She felt as if she had been started from a deep sleep, and a twist of confusion formed across her brow. She shook her head.

"Mom! We gotta go!"

The whine in her son's voice sent a spike of fury into Martha's jaw and she clenched her teeth. The peculiar fog of tiredness had descended on her, proving difficult to shake off. Martha turned quickly from the gaze of the bedroom, childish, stupid fear like the way kids turn uncertainly from the black mouth of some unexplored cave or tunnel. She reached into her messy hair, pulling it into a loose plait she draped around her right shoulder. Her sunglasses were on the dashboard of the other car, they'd hide the lack of makeup because she wasn't going back into that icy stillness.

"You guys ready?" she hollered down the stairs, amazed at the steadiness of her voice.

There were shouts of assent from the children, and Martha descended the small staircase, beginning to hum a bright, warm tune that almost but not quite blocked out the sound of her bedroom door hissing closed across the thick carpet, its tone somehow mocking her, the click of the latch a jeering, guttural giggle.

Martha Walker and her two children stood outside the front door and faced the still green of the forest that surrounded them. The rain that had fallen overnight had turned the single track leading from the cottage onto the narrow, winding road that snaked through the Northumbrian countryside into damp mud. Tire tracks led from where Martin's car had cut through this slight quagmire an hour or so earlier.

Martha, Lauren and Chad were still, staring down from the cottage's front step at the other tracks that had been left in the mud on this damp, English morning.

In almost a perfect circle around Martha Walker's car was a trench, a few inches deep. This ragged circuit was spattered with paw prints inside and out, as if several animals had spent a significant amount of time circling the vehicle. Over five inches long, four-toed and crowned with the triangular treads of pointed claws, these tracks stood out dark and pertinent against the smooth metal of the car.

With the defiance Martha had felt as she had passed the children's landing not half an hour previous, she took their hands and stepped purposefully toward the vehicle.

You're not getting to me.
Not to me, not to us.
No way.

10

No one mentioned the wolf-tracks.

Chad Walker awoke suddenly with this thought stabbing deep into his brain as his need to urinate drove an icy spine into his bladder and forced his eyes open in the darkness.

No one mentioned them. Mom, Dad, Lauren…

Outside, the rain that had greeted them almost as soon as they had exited the car that morning at Alnwick continued to drill a constant barrage against the bedroom windows, and the wind ran shrieking its eerie wail through the trees outside.

Hundreds and thousands of four-toed paw prints had churned up the mud of the track that led from the cottage through the forest until it joined the main road. Like an army of the things had walked the path before them. Or a single one a thousand times.

And nobody mentioned them.

It had been a bad day overall. The visitor-friendly exterior of Alnwick castle had been turned to the fuzzy gray of its distant relative at Blamenholm by the rain. Mist clung to its exterior, the castle appearing more like a looming, blurry shadow. The drained moat around its walls was a dangerous pit of slippery grass that was quickly fenced off with luminous cones by the disgruntled staff. Tourists had been driven inside where their jackets steamed amongst the roped-off paths through the stately home. The graceful magnitude of Alnwick gardens were reduced to pools of standing water. The pivotal water feature, a tiered waterfall structure, had overflowed and sent cascades over its sandblasted sides, drowning the delicate flowers that had begun their life up its banks. The visitors to the gardens, including the Walkers, were ushered out and back onto the winding roads as the wind roared the afternoon into darkness.

The Walker children and their mother had spent the remainder of the day drying off in the cottage. Martin's meeting could potentially last long into the evening, and he had told them not to wait up for him. The children kept to their own bedrooms. Martha flitted between the kitchen and the living room, unwilling to brave the sight of her immaculate bedroom again, preparing an overelaborate meal for the three of them at which they only picked. A defeated quiet seemed to have fallen on the Walkers as the summer sky dissolved into shades of gray and evening fell.

Chad had spent the last few hours as day turned into night in bed, watching old Adam Sandler movies on his laptop. He had grown up with them, and he used their familiar grossness to push against the strange unease that had filled the cottage since their return from the expedition to Alnwick.

That was just pipes thumping from upstairs, that was just a deer brushing through the trees outside. That was just the wind.

Just the wind, the wind, pipes, the wind, the wind.

He must have eventually fallen asleep, and his mother must have come into his room, because the digital display on his phone read 1:15 am and his laptop had been unplugged and tidied away. The blankets of his bed were tucked around his feet, and the curtains had been drawn.

Now though, Chad needed to use the bathroom but sure as eggs is eggs, as his mom would say, there was no way he was setting one foot out of bed right now. It was, perhaps, the disorientation of waking without knowing he had fallen asleep or the remnants of some dream where he ran wildly through trees, their branches whipping at him as he hurtled past. But whatever it was, he felt cold and damp, like he'd been outside... out there in the dark. He shuddered.

The dream did not have that usual frustration, like when his feet were stuck or he was fighting endless, blurred bad guys and his blows were limp and useless. No, in this dream he felt a rush as he charged through the darkness, barely feeling his feet, a curl of pleasure in his stomach along with something else... some *hunger*.

The curtains had been parted about six inches, and from his prostrate position in the bed, Chad could not help but stare at this peculiar gap. If his mother had come in, why would she have done this? They were completely drawn before. Chad straightened up, his eyes still on the gap, listening to the hiss and stammer of the rain against the pane.

He had to look.

Chad did not know why or what he was going to see, but he was drawn to that gap between the curtains. He could feel his own legs lifting him out of his bed, his hands on the cool bed sheets, the pinch of the icy air that seemed to be curling around him as he walked slowly toward that window.

A voice inside Chad was begging him to come back. Just stay in bed there, Chad, don't go looking out that gap 'cause that gap's been put there just for you, kiddo, oh yeah and you know what's gonna happen if you look through that gap, dontcha? Yep, my ol' buddy, some*thing*'s gonna look right back at ya ain't it? Too much Resident Eeeeeeeevil, kiddo, too much...

He could feel his jaw reverberating as his teeth chattered, and what was that? A voice in the drum of the rain, some sounds, some words, a rhythm, a chant.

Arms shaking and the tip of his nose red with the cold, Chad stared through the gap in his curtains into the darkness that called to him.

The waterwheel clung to the side of the cottage, illuminated by the dim light that escaped from one of the windows downstairs. The rain was hammering down on the water that rushed past it, foaming white, the wheel itself black iron, its spokes thick cylinders. Chad was mesmerized by the sight of it, and he gazed upon the ancient thing as the rain screamed down from the ink black of the night sky.

That's when it began, the howls—those great cries that whistled and boomed—like the strange, lonely voices of whales. Chad could feel the hairs on his arms and the back of his neck raise taut and gooseflesh prickle his skin, which had nothing to do with the cold.

It reminded him of being lost in the dark of some museum when he was a little kid. His dad had to take a phone call and Chad had not seen him leave. Suddenly he had been alone in the darkness, staring up at the gargantuan, slightly faded coils of a giant squid wrapped around the blue underbelly of a whale. It was a corny exhibition, but Chad had only been about six and the piped-in wails of these sea behemoths had echoed around the gloom and filled him with awe that swiftly turned to fear.

The howls he heard now brought back the panic, the *vastness* of that dark museum all those years ago, when all around him were illuminated tanks of still, long-dead sea life and his dad was nowhere to be seen. Voices and visions rallied from somewhere far in the trees and brought with them smells—a feeling of something ancient, something that stared from far away with searching eyes and a voice that was the howl of a

66

thousand wolves, crying, crying like they were hurt and they needed him.

Another mighty howl began again, and Chad almost buckled at the pain it carried. Both hands were planted on the pane of the window as he stared out into the darkness and that was the moment he felt his jaw go slack and a shiver come thundering through him from the tips of his toes to the ends of his fingers. The ancient waterwheel began to turn, its metal screaming and its paddles lapping hungrily at the water beneath it.

Chad could feel tears pouring down his face as the howls hung in the night air, weaving in and out of the rain, coming from nowhere and everywhere, inside and out all at once. The great wheel picked up speed and slapped at the water frantically. The whine of the ancient metal carried the long pain that hung in those howls. The howling was joined by a rough cawing, the rusty voices of tattered black birds. You remember those birds, right, Chad? Dontcha?

Yeah, that old movie that Lauren let you watch when she was supposed to be babysitting you, that one that never really left your head. There's that bit where those little kids have gotta cross that schoolyard and those hundreds of birds are just sat on the jungle gym, just *waiting* for them. You remember that now, Chad, dontcha? Sat on the sofa which felt suddenly cold and exposed as you watched those little kids running and that sound, the screech of the crows, the screams of the kids and the unholy beat of the wings as they came at them again and again with their sharp, black beaks. You know what the scariest part of it was though, Chad, the part that got to you most, was the fact that even the adults were scared, the mommies and daddies and the teachers, they were running too and they were screaming. They were *screaming*.

Chad could stand it no more. The pain angled through him, filling his head with a torturous, childish fear he could barely comprehend. He broke his gaze from the water wheel and closed his eyes. A shiver scythed through him, and he took one last look out of the window, a horror pile-driving its muddy way into his stomach, nearly releasing his brimming bladder as the sight of something swinging from the branches of one of the pale trees that surrounded the cottage caught his gaze. It was horribly tall and thin, with a tattered cloak that whipped raggedly in the wind and rain that brushed the ground below its feet as the branches of the trees bowed with the wind. But it was the face that chilled Chad to his very innards. From some fold in the cloak, a single, furious eye glared up at the house, very much alive and brimming with hate. Two monstrous birds flew down to the swinging body, screeching in their iron tongue before the wind changed direction and the trees lurched the other way. The swinging body and the birds fell out of sight and the waterwheel sat as still as it had always been.

Chad closed his curtains and fell, shaking, into bed.

11

Lauren Walker was wrenched suddenly from sleep by the trill of her cell phone. The vibration of the handset against the wood of her bedside table was the furious fizzing of a trapped hornet, almost drowning the shrill polyphonies of her ringtone. Such was the suddenness of her awakening from what must have been a deep sleep, her whole body seemed to reel along with her mind.

She was confused, disconcerted and somehow furious about someone even thinking of calling her right now. There was a time difference of eight hours, but they should know that. Struggling from the soft tentacles of what must have been a "deep ol' slumberoo" as her dad would have put it on the times he occasionally decided to be at home and was there in the mornings when she came downstairs, all big grins. What's that, Dad? Another new laptop for me? Well gee thanks, and what's that? Off to Europe tomorrow, again?

Her tongue felt thick and furry, and the frantic light of the buzzing phone was making her squint. The rain was yammering on the window and the wind was whining balefully.

It stopped.

Suddenly all Lauren could hear was her heart, the yowl of the weather was now only background noise. She felt her breath coming, heavy, lifting her shoulders. She stared down at her phone that was thankfully still, quiet but for an accusatory red light that blinked impatiently.

Hey! It seemed to say *Hey, you, yeah you... someone called, hey! Someone called! You hear me?*

"Yeah," Lauren whispered, "I know." But there was something inside her that resisted, something that repelled her hand from picking up the phone, turning it over and finding out that sure, it was only Bevvie or Suzie with something that was *ohmygodyougottahearthis* gossip-tastic and would end in an *isitreallythattimeoverthere*? Fit of giggles and despite herself, despite the time and the fright they had given her, Lauren would giggle along too.

But there was something, a cold weight in her stomach that seemed to know that it'd be far, far from a stupid mistake by one of her friends. Oh no, whatever—whomever—had called her at this time in the morning knew exactly what they... it was doing. That cold in her stomach was fear, a terrible fear as that little light winked at her.

With a shaking hand, Lauren reached into the suddenly ice-cold air with a trembling hand. This heavy dread quaking silently at the pit of her stomach was familiar, all too familiar.

In the milliseconds before her fingers made contact with her phone, it began to ring again, making Lauren shriek, curling her fingers as if from the sudden thrum of an electric current.

"You don't scare me..." Her breath fogged in the cold, and the words felt so insincere. She might as well have said nothing.

The display read *Unknown Number*.

Of course it did. She picked up the phone, the wind screeching at her through the miniscule gaps in the frame of the window.

As her thumb moved automatically to the green icon on the touch screen, the howling desisted, holding its breath of anticipation.

"Hello." Lauren kept her voice calm, kept it strong.

You don't scare me. "Yeah? Hello?" Lauren's voice was tight with sleep. Her tongue felt dry and sticky against the roof of her mouth.

Nothing from the other end, just a vague crackle and what felt like the merest hint of breathing.

Lauren's hands had started to tremble and her own breath came in small puffs of vapor, yet she did not seem to notice the spur of ice that had begun to coat the air with the sickening drop in temperature. The room suddenly seemed larger and darker than it was, the walls peeling back and vanishing, the childish idea of things that lurked in the dark places Lauren's throat almost closing in terror as the silence that hung on the other end of the phone line hung like some ancient, dead weight.

This was the girls, this had to be the girls. The time-difference was all messed up and maybe they were playing a joke, some trick. They were at school, they knew it was the middle of the night and soon, someone would whisper "You'll die in seven days," amid stifled giggles.

But the dead silence at the other end of the phone did not feel like a trick.

Lauren's friends did not play those sorts of tricks.

"Hello." This time it was a whisper, Lauren's eyes had swum out of focus and the world lurched around her, walls and furniture traipsing in gray shadows.

"Hey, Lauren…" The voice whirled from Lauren's phone in an ethereal bubble of static, like a poor imitation of human speech from some obsolete computer.

She did not notice, but the last two fingers on her right hand that held her phone had changed from red to an almost lavender shade of purple, through a combination of cold and her grasp on the phone.

Lauren could feel tears trickling from the corners of her eyes, tightening to ice on her cheeks.

Lauren had first begun having trouble sleeping at around the time she had begun fourth grade. Martin and Martha had noticed it when Lauren had begun getting ill. She had never been a sickly child and had always relished her days in the classroom, bounding eagerly from the front gates at the end of the day into her mother's car to give a breathless, smiling commentary about what had occurred. Lauren was bright and more often than not received high grades, something of which she was proud but not boastful. Martha speculated to herself that perhaps it was undue pressure to achieve that Lauren had put on herself when she began developing "headaches" and a "sore tummy" on Monday mornings. When these ailments began carrying on into Tuesdays and sometimes Wednesdays, Lauren always pale and listless but with no fever or other physical symptoms of illness, Martha's motherly intuition began to alert her that something was not all it seemed.

Martha had gone into her daughter's bedroom late one night and found Lauren hunched in a knot at the foot of her bed, amidst a small snowdrift of crumpled kitchen paper, her face wrinkled with tears.

It had all come out that morning. Lauren finally confided in her mother, as the sun rose gradually over Huntleigh County, what had been keeping her staring at the ceiling, her stomach churning and eyes brimming with unadulterated misery in those lonely hours before she had to wake for school.

Casey Dodds was her name. Coils of impossibly glossy, black curls seemed to bounce around her shoulders as she walked, her face trowel-deep in orange foundation and the delicate pink of her lips curled in a permanent sneer. Lauren's stomach felt tight whenever she had to walk within Casey's eye-shot in the halls or at recess. Heavy and thick with mascara, they seemed to glare at Lauren in unbridled fury which sent fear racing through her, her mouth drying instantly and breath coming in short, sharp gulps. Lauren had *sensed* this dislike, smelled it on the air like a half-wild dog.

The inevitable happened, half-whispered, inaudible comments as Lauren walked past, the shrieking and cackling of Casey's friends made Lauren's cheeks burn.

"She *di'int* just look at me?" in a high tone of mock-outrage came next, no matter how careful Lauren was to avoid Casey's hungry gaze.

"I'd slap the shit outta that bitch if she be lookin' at me like that, *girrrrrrrl.*" A parting comment from some friend of Casey as Lauren walked past, head down, hair hanging limply over her face and all Lauren could think of was *No, please just leave me alone, please.*

Glue all over her bag, spit all over her coat, spit-balls of mushed paper in her hair and it was every day, every single day.

"I think she just hates me," Lauren had sobbed into her mother's shoulder, "and I don't know why, Mom, what did I do?"

Dissolving into tears again, Martha had not needed to ask whether this question had kept her daughter awake at night, staring into the shadows, a lead weight of fear buried deep in her stomach and a tirade of insults from this girl whirring through her mind.

Lauren had not thought about Casey for years, the outcome of telling her mom all that time ago was that Martha had gone to the school, spoken to the principal and something had been done. Lauren had never asked what had happened, but Casey never even gave her so much as a snide glance again.

Until now.

Another burst of static muffled the reply, her mind echoed her response. It couldn't be, there's no way it could be—but Jesus Holy Christ it was and there was no mistake. That loathsome sneer in her voice, the feel of claw-like false nails in a slap against her face, Casey Dodds out of nowhere cornering her by the drinking fountain again. Casey Dodds holding her head onto the freezing porcelain where a million kids had spat. Casey Dodds shrieking her sour laughter as cold water cascaded into Lauren's hair.

Wash your face, you dirty little dyke.

A gurgling chuckle accompanied by a burst of static came over the phone, and this time the voice did not even sound human, it was the rusted spines of pure hatred that sent a huge hiccupping sob through Lauren as she shivered beside her bed, the light of the DAB radio faint now with the ice that was beginning to form across its surface.

"What do you want?" Lauren managed, and there was another hissing breath.

"I'll find you, Lauren…" For a fleeting second as Casey Dodd's voice breathed in, the static on the line was halted, then, as she breathed out again, it returned with an ear-splitting crackle. "Wherever you go, I'll find you… "

With a choked screech, Lauren Walker hurled her phone into one of the black pockets of her room, hearing it shatter against some surface, the hissing, mocking giggle dissipating gradually as Lauren curled into a ball with her head under the pillow and sobbed herself back to sleep.

12

The high beams of headlights lit the road in an eerie gold light, along with the dry stone walls and hedgerows that flanked it. The vehicle wound around the coils and thundered down the dips as Martin Walker cut his route home through the desolate countryside. He was dressed in his tailored suit, the collar loosened and tie removed, his feet finding the vehicle's pedals easily through his walnut brown Italian loafers. From the conference center in Alnwick, along this slim road back to the cottage, Martin had not passed another vehicle or a single pedestrian. The countryside whirred by, hedgerows rising and falling alongside him like waves.

He could vaguely see the forest approaching in the distance, the vast lines of trees, a legion of swaying, ebon soldiers. No streetlamps lit the road and the foot-high reflective road markers were only in place in the most angular of corners. He did not have the radio on, his full concentration was focused on the route ahead. Despite the mangled corpses of rabbits, hedgehogs, and the crumpled balls of feathers that had once been pheasants, nothing rushed from the hedgerows in front of his car. This lonely, now familiar drive was his and his alone. As Martin wound his way from yet another slow-moving and ultimately frustrating meeting concerning the Gateway development on Blamenholm, he was reflecting on not only the day that had passed, but the peculiar fortnight as a whole.

Today's disaster was some sort of corruption on the files from the architect which contained the finalized designs for the Gateway structure that would be built in place of the castle. Despite every member of the Gateway development team having been emailed the documents (which had worked perfectly the previous evening), an infuriating error message appeared when anyone attempted to open them. Martin had somehow managed to keep a lid on the fury that was drilling its white-hot fingernails into his skull, but in his head he picked up the computers and smashed them again and again into the faces of the technical team. Just looking at their frustration and the ludicrous error messages that flooded the screen made him want to roar with rage.

The morning had been spent on a conference call to tech-support, which kept cutting out. Eventually, one of the laptops blue-screened and Martin's lost all battery power, his charger turning out not to be in the case, his bag, the car boot, nor the back seat, despite the fact he remembered clearly putting it in the case this morning.

The memory of the day's frustration irked Martin still; he clenched his jaw and tightened his grip on the steering wheel, staring dead ahead at the road. The rain had begun again, falling lazily in a fine mist. With a deft flick of his little finger, Martin activated the windshield wipers. Their arc cleared the fog of the rain for an instant, but in that instant Martin almost slammed on the brakes and sent his car sliding across the wet road into a short dry stone wall. In one of the desolate fields that flanked the road and rolled into the horizon, something had *moved*. It was not the movement that disturbed him—Martin was used to wildlife and strived to work alongside it as best he could with his resorts—it was the *way* it had moved that chilled him, a lolloping bipedal stagger across the field.

Slowing slightly, Martin craned his neck to stare out across the inky blackness of the countryside but saw nothing more. He shook his head and regained focus on the road as the single-lane track that led into the forest was coming up on his left. The stress of the last fortnight was clearly getting to him. That and the lack of sleep. Why did the kids insist on behaving in such an immature way? He and Martha were forever being woken by the sound of them tearing up and down their corridor. No wonder they looked so tired. "Let them be," Martha had said. "Kids adapt to change in their own ways."

With the development plans for the resort designs eighty-sixed, Martin had begun proceedings to find a local contractor firm to quote him for the eventual excavation of the wreckage of Blamenholm's outer walls, the keep and the leveling of the land. Short-tempered after the morning's unproductiveness, Martin had waved away, testily, the rest of the Gateway team's concerns about the demolition of the place.

"We're being hypothetical here, people!" Martin snarled, uncharacteristically aggressive as he had been every time the subject of the castle's fate had been brought up. "But I promise you, they'll be *glad* to be rid of the place."

Martin Walker felt a sort of grim pleasure in the thought of excavating that hateful building, digging out its roots the way one would destroy a wart.

Flipping on the turn signal, more as force of habit than anything else (there were no other vehicles to be seen for miles around), Martin turned the car onto the track that led into the forest. As the wall of trees closed, sentry-like behind the vehicle, it began its ascent through the winding gravel track alongside the rush of Wooler Water five or so miles to the cottage, Martin gave a sigh. The strange sight in the field, which must have definitely been his imagination, had unsettled him. He clicked on the radio and winced as only white nose burst at a horribly intrusive volume from the speakers.

Slowing the car to a halt, Martin cringed from the racket that was blaring inside the vehicle. He flicked frantically at the dials and switches but nothing seemed to affect the screech of static that assaulted his ears. In a rage, Martin slapped, open-handed, at the dashboard. That's when everything stopped.

The engine cut out, and the headlamps blinked off. Rattling the key in the ignition did no good. The vehicle *felt* lifeless. Martin gave a groan and began fumbling impatiently in his pocket for his iPhone. Luckily he knew more or less where he was and if it came to it, he wasn't far from the cottage. With no light in the car, nor on the road, he was in virtually pitch blackness. The only sound was the steady rush of rain against the windows. Martin's phone indicated a new message, and the small glow from the touchscreen was most welcome. The phone's screen lit up Martin's face, and he noticed with some confusion that his breath had begun to steam. He gave a shiver as he noticed the icy air in the car, which, as if acknowledging him back, began to prick at him. Looking down at his phone, Martin opened his text messages and was given his second start of the evening.

The number of the sender was blank, and the body of the message was two words.

GET HOME

It screamed up at him. The sight sent a spear of terror into Martin's stomach. If the message had read "Go home," somehow, it would have felt easier to stomach, more of a warning, less of a command.

The simple substitution of the word sounded more... direct... as if the last chance had gone.

He stared down at the message and the blank number, suddenly very afraid. He knew he must call Martha, get the road service to come fix the car, but he couldn't trust his hands not to shake and could not compose the right words in his head to explain the fear he was feeling, the trepidation.

Get home.

The imperative stayed burned into Martin's retina as he tried to key to the car again. It turned with a faint crunch yet induced nothing more. Did those ominous words correspond to now, were they a warning to find a way off this lonely woodland road and return to the cottage? To Martin, the message seemed more substantial. *Get home*, get out of here, go back to the States and leave well alone. Martin replaced his phone to the inner pocket of his jacket. Taking a deep breath, he placed two hands on the steering wheel of the car and stared forward into the night in an attempt to compose himself.

Martin let out an involuntary, girlish squeak from somewhere at the back of his throat when something banged on the roof of the car.

He had seen enough made-for-television cop movies in which a fugitive escapes the locked traffic of a jammed freeway by turning tail on foot and leaping onto the roofs of halted vehicles. It was that heavy crunch of something landing, two-footed on the roof of the car that had made him start. He stared frantically over his right shoulder to the inside of the car's roof, half-expecting to see twin indentations protruding inward. There was nothing.

The temperature inside the car dropped again and Martin was breathing quicker, clouding and steaming up the windows. A steady fear thrummed through him, clawing at the walls of his stomach and he felt tears pricking helplessly in his eyes. There was something or someone on the roof of the car. They—*it*—had jumped from somewhere and was now motionless atop the roof.

With trembling fingers, Martin rubbed his fingers against the door locks, making sure they were all depressed. There were movements now on both sides, where trees bent with age blocked out the sky. Martin, shivering, peered into the gloom, wiping gently at the condensation that hung like a dense cobweb over the inside of the windscreen.

Through the darkness, Martin could make out movements from within the trees, things were gliding effortlessly between branches, great bipedal shadows that clung to the branches and swung silently before vanishing into the blackness. Martin clasped a hand over his mouth and he felt a surge of adrenaline tear through him sending his flesh scurrying across his bones in shivers. More of the silent, ape-like shadows were flitting through the trees in the direction he had been travelling, toward the cottage. Martin gave a roar of pure terror and frantically turned the key in the car again and again, tears now coursing down his face as the swinging shadows were slowing, turning their shaggy black heads to regard the car, lamp-like eyes glaring malevolently in long, leathery faces, jagged teeth bared in growls of baleful hate.

The engine stirred, and the headlights illuminated the strip of gravel path that led into the forest. Ragged, shrieking breaths emanated from Martin Walker. Somehow he managed to rev the engine and launch the vehicle forward. There was a scraping sound from the roof, the sound of talons against metal, and whatever it was that had been atop the roof leapt, howling into the darkness of the trees. Martin screamed out loud as he saw its matted silhouette, easily eight feet tall and jumping chimp-like into the trees. He floored the accelerator, spurred by pure fear, seeing nothing but the road rearing in front of him until driving was too much for him to handle any longer. The car screeched to a halt, and Martin Walker curled in the driving seat, sobbing for all he was worth.

13

When the light of the morning began peering through the trees and streaming through the windshield, breathing color into the leaves and turning the branches from black to brown, Martin Walker dared to open his eyes.

His phone read that it was around 8 am and that he had received no text messages, nor emails all night. In fact, the phone had completely reset, there were no numbers, emails, texts or applications saved whatsoever.

Martin stared down at the phone screen, rubbing at his eyes and licking his lips that were dry and cracked from the tears, his throat raw from his screams.

It must have been a dream.

The meeting must have gone on too late.

I was too tired, I pulled over because it's dangerous to drive when you're tired.

It says so on the commercials.

It was a dream.

A terrible, terrible dream.

Martin returned to the cottage, his footsteps deliberate, quiet, as he unlocked the door amidst the faint tweeting of birds from the forest.

He did not look at the side of the house.

The side of the house where the long-still waterwheel now turned silently.

He did not look at the roof of the house.

The roof of the house that was no longer visible through a crumpled carpet of hooded crows that followed his every footfall with the points of their beaks and their bobbing heads.

With every breath he took, he felt the furious gaze of the monocular eye that regarded him from the trees, recalled the limp, tattered body that hung in a ragged, black cloak.

He found his children slumbering beside his wife in the main bedroom. After carrying them each back to their own bedrooms, he lay down next to his wife, the bed warm from their bodies.

GET HOME.

14

The dining table in the mill cottage was large and round, made from thick English oak with an unblemished finish. A large teapot sat in the center in place of where the Walker's would usually have coffee. Serving bowls were filled with sausages and bacon, the china toast rack filled with thick granary toast. A jug of orange juice stood beside a plate of steaming Belgian waffles and a small bottle of maple syrup.

Outside, the morning was stifled by a mass of slate-gray clouds that were already spitting a churlish fret of streaky rain against the windows.

Martin Walker sat before his family with a face ominous as a thunderhead.

"I'm gonna ask just one more time and I want you guys to be honest with me, okay?"

His eyes were dark. Great bags stood out on his usually youthful features.

Martha looked tired too, her face free of makeup and her hair coiled on top of her head in a loose bun. Dressed in their robes, their faces creased from sleep, Lauren and Chad were slumped at the breakfast table, barely able to keep their eyes open.

"Which one of you has been messing with my laptop… my phone? Just fess up, okay?"

There was silence from the breakfast table. The midday sun shone in through the large windows and the green forest outside swayed slightly.

"Listen… " Martin's voice faltered slightly as he stared around at his family and the untouched food in front of them.

"I know things are… strange right now… "

At this, there was an audible thump from somewhere on the floor above them. The family jumped simultaneously, and Chad looked back and forth to his parents, eyes wide and glazed with the beginnings of tears.

Martin, wincing at the sound, continued, "We're in a strange country, a strange place, it's not home, I know… "

Lauren too, looked like she was holding back tears. Her head slumped forward, propped up by one hand.

"But we just have to pull together for a little while until things are… "

One of the doors upstairs slammed shut. The Walkers ignored it. Martin continued, his teeth gritted.

"…until things are sorted and the building work begins…"

The Blamenholm budget had gone from bullshit to a total clusterfuck. Every day a new cost swelled from somewhere unexpected, red raw like some out of control infection. Gateway simply did not have the money for the project. Martin did not have the money he owed for his cars, his staff, even his damn *suits* for chrissakes because there was no way in hell he was going to that office every day and telling them he had failed. The corporate bookings for the resorts across the states were fading like flies, the Internet was raging with complaints about the shoddy maintenance and inflated prices. The company was spending the best part of their time fire-fighting, keeping the reviewers quiet, laying on free weekends for journalists, hell even bloggers were getting a night in the goddamn forests if they had more than a hundred followers.

He would not tell them he had failed. This had to succeed. There was no way back.

"Dad… " Lauren started, but he ignored her.

Keep it together. Keep it in auto-Mart.

"Stealing my laptop, messing about with my phone is only going to slow the process…"

And when the last meeting ended yesterday in this freezing pocket of Northern England, Martin had stood at the window watching the final wisp of exhaust from the car of the last investor disappear into the pale air.

As final as the guy's muttered, guilty apology as he left, leaving Martin alone in the office.

"Dad. Stop." Lauren was sobbing now, Chad was shaking his head, his hands over his ears.

A thumping began from what sounded like it came from inside the wall to their right, with each word, it got louder but Martin doggedly continued, raising his own voice.

"But when—that's right—when, not if this project is finished…"

Pushing his chair back, Martin stood, turning his head to the ceiling as if addressing the heavens.

"When the project is finished, when that place is destroyed, all this will *go away*!"

Martin's final two words resonated back and forth in a sudden echo, as if the kitchen had expanded into a vast hall. Chad and Lauren clutched at Martha who held her arms around them fierce and protective, her neck taut like a mother swan.

There was a sudden, tense silence in the kitchen as the echoes of Martin's exclamation died away. The air ran cold and the soiled scent of old stone began to fill the air. Were there other sounds filtering into that frosted silence too? The crash of waves, the aching caw of seagulls and was that the creak of sails?

Another collective start from the Walkers as another thump came from upstairs, louder this time, but it was the noise that followed that sent them staring, wide-eyed at each other.

It was the little gasping tone that signaled Martin's MacBook had been roused. The sound was very loud and slightly distorted, as if the volume had been turned up to maximum.

Martin ran from the kitchen and took the stairs two at a time, past the landing where, if he'd looked down the short corridor, he would have seen both children's bedroom doors wide open. His mind, however, was racing.

It was a prank, it *had* to be a prank. Of course that's what it was. Kids these days know more about technology than adults ever will, we're just playing catch up while they're out there in the end zone with the ball. Chad or Lauren had sent some signal with their phone.

Martin thundered into the bedroom on the top floor of the cottage, screeching to a halt like Wiley Coyote in one of those old cartoons. His MacBook open on the bed, its screen facing him, displaying a full-screen image that he couldn't quite see from where he was standing in the doorway. As Martin advanced on the screen that sat before him, the image open on it was dark and blurred, giving it the look of a glaring, black eye that stared furiously at him as he stood before the bed.

That's when Martin realized just how cold the bedroom had become. There were more noises outside too, the crash of the waves and that creaking which had gotten louder. If the blinds of the window were not closed, Martin would have not been surprised to see a fleet of tall ships with billowing sails creaking in the wind, collected at the shore of the distant coastline.

Anger was building inside Martin. They had managed it all right, his family had scared him, he was a big enough man to admit that, but *why*? It didn't matter. It was clear the investors were not going to support the Blamenholm Gateway project, but what did they know? The kids had some bullshit romance with that hateful place. Martha had done nothing but moan since they'd got to England. Did they have any idea how hard he'd worked for this? Did they have any idea of what would happen if the Blamenholm project fell through? It would be no more fancy private education, no more house with a pool, none of the things that he and he alone had provided for them and that they didn't seem to give two shits about. The Walkers would end up like every other schmuck in the country who plodded along in the rat race, counting the pennies. He'd end up like every other fool with a dream.

He did not know it, but his fists were clenched, his knuckles white, his fingernails grinding into his palms.

The blurred JPEG image that filled his screen was what looked like a candid photograph from that vile entrance hall inside Blamenholm castle.

So that's what his family thought of him.

GET HOME

Hazy and desperate.

GET

Full of nothing but emptiness and hate.

HOME

"Never," Martin whispered to himself through clenched teeth, the roar of anger inside his head meeting the crash of those waves to reach a splintering, guttural crescendo.

15

The estimated cost of the demolition of the place was escalating almost hourly. The nearby Farne islands were protected wildlife sanctuaries—there was no way they could simply fill Blamenholm with dynamite and blast the place into the North Sea. Gateway was a *green* business, though back home a green business meant if you took down some trees, you just made sure no one was watching. There was also debate over which *parish* or some bullshit *committee* was responsible for the maintenance of the castle's disposal. English freaking Heritage were sniffing about too, trying to decide if the place was listed. They hadn't cared about the fucking place being listed when it had stood empty and boarded up for all those years had they? The papers Martin had obtained from Blamenholm's previous owners, the fucking deeds to the place, the certificate of ownership, were worthless.

And why could he not get hold of Saul? The only guy in the entire freaking place who could help, his number didn't seem to work anymore. It just rang and rang, no voicemail, no nothing. Martin had sat for an hour at four o'clock till five in the morning, his phone warm against his face, grinding his teeth until his molars were coated with a terrible sandy dust, listening to Saul's phone ring and ring. As each minute passed, his teeth creaking to the steady burr of the phone and the sound of his wife's heavy breathing beside him, he imagined a room, an empty room with an old fashioned telephone with one of those brass dials, and each time it rung, the handset vibrated, shaking dust from it like dandruff. All Martin wanted to do was take that telephone and hurl it to the ground, watching it shatter before him, its innards spilling across the cold, carpet-less floor in a hundred thousand pieces.

Martin jumped.

His body lurched with the sudden hypnogogic twitch and he was wide awake and standing in the bedroom of the mill cottage, staring at the screen of the MacBook that sat open on his bed. It was a surreal moment, Martin had not been asleep, nor even in that trance-like state he called *auto-Mart* that he found himself in when he was alone in his office after working too many hours. One moment he had been filled to the brim with an ungodly fury that he felt at the back of his clenched teeth, all sorts of images and impulses had come whizzing through his mind, the predominant being the desire to express his rage on... his wife... Martin's face burned red at the simple thought of it... his *kids?* Then it had gone and he had twitched himself what? Awake?

Martin slowly became aware of the passage of time before he became aware of the silence in the cottage. Outside, the clouds were thick in a gray sky and the windows of the cottage were lashed with rain. The blinds of the window had been opened... he had opened them. He had to have done it. He had no idea what time of day it was, but time had definitely passed. The quiet of the cottage swam to the forefront of his mind.

There is no silence in an empty place like the silence of a house that is occupied but quiet. Martin felt an odd chill scamper across his forearms as he strained his ears to hear a noise, any noise from down the stairs where his family... *was?* Panic gripped his belly in an icy fist and the world lurched around him. The sound of the waves crashed from what seemed like all around, as if the cottage was marooned in the middle of some raging sea. Within that crash of the waves came a great creaking, the splintering groan of cold bones turning arthritically in sockets that pained his eyes closed and set his teeth on edge.

A horrible image filled his mind: slate-blue waves that rose relentlessly in icy crests of foam, bearing something that bobbed at their peaks, cutting through the swell. It was a ship, an ancient longboat the grimy yellow of old bones with a great sail that hung from bent, creaking masts. The sound of the foul craft bobbed heavily upon the water, sending uncontrollable shivers up and down his arms. He tried to open his eyes, the sight of that ship sending splinters of freezing fear and revulsion into his belly, but the noise of it kept coming. As the wind whipped its ragged black sails high onto the crest of a wave, Martin could see its foul, curving dragon-head, forged from hundreds of long, horse-like skulls, a crown of curling horns at its head. Its prow was encrusted with a pox of long-dead barnacles and spiny limpet shells.

"No," Martin whispered. The stench of rotten death filled his nostrils, bile burning at the back of his throat.

The ship of bones began to turn, its hull visible for a second through the waves as it beat a starboard course away from his mind's eye. Martin felt sick rising in him as he gaped at the foul vessel. Clumps of matted hair held what looked like scales cutting through the froth of the sea, which Martin knew were not scales but thousands upon thousands of finger- and toenails, their stumps brown with ancient blood from the feet and fingers of which they had been ripped. He forced his fingertips into his ears as the creaking from the longboat's hull and sails ripped through him, sending him rolling across the plush carpet of the bedroom.

That's when the voice came.

It did not come from above, nor below, nor from either side, it just seemed to be. The voice was an ancient, grating snarl that could be felt in the air, warm like breath and reeking of long-rotten sea weed and hollow shells.

"GET HOME!" Its voice was a thousand shrieking sea birds.

Martin began to sob, "This can't be happening, it just *can't,"* before exploding into a rumbling, spiteful laughter that shook the glasses in the cupboards and sent Martin crashing to his knees. The thrum of wings sounded from outside as a great cloud of startled ravens rose from the roof, and the gravel of the drive and clattering through the air, before vanishing into the trees, their rusty voices reverberating long after they were crooked black specks in the sky.

Martin's hands clamped, vise-like on each side of his head to protect his ears and he heaved himself to his feet.

Martha.

The children.

Paroxysms of fear shuddered through him as he stumbled, drunkenly out through the bedroom door and down the short flight of stairs to the first floor bedroom landing. He hadn't noticed the open doors on his ascent, but by Christ he saw what had happened now.

A trail of thick, peat-black dirt screamed out from the pale of the carpet that led past huge tears in the paint on the walls of either side. Both doors hung from their shattered frames, Chad's door broken nearly in half. Martin stopped again to stare, a churning horror beginning in his stomach.

There was no fucking way to be rational about this—what, not who but what—had done this? Those rips in the wall, which have opened like wounds to show the wood, the filth that lead in cruel curves into Chad and Lauren's bedrooms, the rooms of his babies.

And you had to do it, Walker, my man, didn't you? As soon as you came up against an obstacle you went head-down, full on charge, yeah, lets blow the shit out of a thousand years of miserable history and burn that island to the ground and you know why didn't you? It was because they loved it, your kids, your wife, those three others that flitted in and around your life like ghosts when you have the time for them, when you're not closing the deals, *blowing those little fish outta the water* and stamping your brand, taming the wild places of the world. You wanted to take the place apart from the inside and build it again as yours didn't you? Well, Walker, one of those wild places didn't want to be tame and look what it took from you.

There was no denying it, there was no bowing to the rational at this moment because the trail of mud that led through the house and the splintered wood where once there had been door frames, that was Blamenholm, with paws, black with the stagnant peat that grew on its shores, Blamenholm that had sat alone with its terrible echoes of terrible things replaying endlessly against its walls, pacing back and forth like some starved animal, just waiting for something, for someone to reach close enough to bite. Someone like him.

With the leaden steps of defeat, Martin descended the stairs, his feet dragging in the matted mud of the carpet. When he reached the kitchen, he began to hear the distant hiss of the waves again and the creak of that foul ship.

"No… no…"

Something gradually dawned on Martin as he stepped through the hole in the wall, where there had once been a kitchen door, and into the small garden where the bird table lay in half. Above, the clouds were gathered in a snarl as evening began to swell across the land.

He knew, oh God he knew that somehow in some fucked-up, impossible way that it was Martha and Chad and Lauren aboard that ship and that its foul, dragon-headed prow was cutting through the waves to take them to the keep, to swallow them in the black dungeon of that place. Just as he'd sworn he'd rip Blamenholm's wretched heart out from the inside, Blamenholm had sworn it would take everything from him for even considering it.

And it laughed. The voice rose an octave, spikes of sound as it spat spiteful howls of mirth into the still defiance of the bedroom. As if in answer to this terrible noise, the skies above the cottage opened and the rain began to lash down in a vicious torrent. All across the costal flats of Northumberland, the beaches and woodland paths turned to mush as the skies belched their wars upon the earth. The North Sea reared white heads of rage as the wind tore across its surface. Martin screamed up at the sky as the laughter and thunder intertwined into a hideous rumbling.

"You won't beat me!" Martin screamed at the gloom of the horizon where the blue of the whale-road began. "I'm coming for them, you fuck, and I will get them back. Then I will rip out your cold, dead heart and raze you…"

"...to the ground," Robert Milburn's voice was sour, "while we had the chance."

"Ah, save your tears man," Walter Milburn growled. "What's done is done."

Robert stood at the prow of the small boat, staring purposefully forward, his back to the island and castle that eventually diminished and sank over the horizon. His brother stood beside him, his gaze occasionally flickering to the craft's stern, where blazed a white trail of sea fret that trod the course of the Reivers' exit from Blamenholm. The remaining men aboard the craft were quiet, busying themselves with the sail or staring from the ship into the approaching dawn as it cut through the still waters of the North Sea.

"You're sure they took not a stone from that place?" Robert muttered to the teeth of the wind that whirled around them and gestured behind him at the men without turning his head.

"Nothing." Walter was grim. His eyes and slight tremble in his set bottom lip betrayed the fear that still lingered amongst the Reivers on board since their attempt on Blamenholm's walls.

He was scared, still scared. So would any man who had seen what he thought he—no, what he knew he saw—what he'd swear on his own blood he saw in that ungodly place. The men were scared too. It was only their few numbers and weariness that had stopped them turning tail and flying as soon as they saw... when they heard...

"Holy Island is in sight!"

The cry came from further down the vessel. One of the men was pointing at a faint speck on the horizon, *only just visible in the eerie blue phosphorescence of the dawn. Walter was disgusted at the high relief he heard on the man's voice and was about to bark his derision, but he felt his brother's hand fall lightly upon his shoulder.*

"Stay silent, brother," Robert's voice was soft, "for madness we cannot tempt."

Walter made to swipe at Robert's hand but thought better of it and instead grunted to the men.

"Turn us starboard! We land at Lindisfarne by daybreak!"

He turned back to Robert who still stared into the distance where the blue of the sea rose in small, white crests and flocks of wailing birds rose and fell in vast swoops to its surface.

"What was it, Robert?" Walter said, his voice hoarse, eyes furtive for listening ears from the men. "What devil dwells in the black keep of Blamenholm?"

Robert did not answer at first, his shoulders rose and fell and his head tipped forward, the only sound the rattle of his cloak with the wind.

"It was a morning, not unlike this one when the English marched on Berwick," Robert began, his voice hollow with a desperate horror.

Walter spat, his tongue making a dry click against his palate and he shook his head.

"I'll no hear that tale once more, brother," he growled, following Robert's gaze into the horizon as the boat's prow began to turn against the flow of the tide and the wind caught with a whump in the tattered sail.

"Longshanks will claim his rightful seat in hell for what he done to that place, mark my words."

Robert was unperturbed by his brother and began to sing, gently in a lilting half-voice that seemed to harmonize with the wail of the wind.

"Row, row with steel and fury in your hearts me boys / Row, row from the island of bones / For no man, no woman no bairn will see morn / While we reap like the wolf-men of old Blamenholm... "

"Stop it, Robert."

"Come with the axe, the blade and the bow / Spread the black sail o'er the land as we go / No Scot will live to sing the tale of the blood gift / We lay at the feet of the gods of below... "

"I said stop it!" Walter halted his brother's song, clutching hard at his shoulder.

"Seven men escaped Berwick that day, brother, seven men from a whole town," Robert whispered, his teeth gritted.

"Longshanks hung six of them from the trees at Chillingham as food for birds and beasts, the last remained, wandering the roads, a madman."

The Holy Isle of Lindisfarne was now visible ahead of the boat, the curved roof of the monastery silhouetted against the orange blaze of the rising sun.

"I spoke with this last man, the sole survivor of that day." Robert grasped Walter's shoulder again and spoke into his face, his eyes wide, lip trembling. "He said the English did not march on land as the tales tell, but sailed from Blamenholm, that their ships rode before a pagan vessel, the size of which he had never seen."

"Speak no more," Walter gasped, "not in sight of God's... "

"He said aboard that black ship stood creatures of unspeakable foulness, brother."

A small gathering of cowl-clad monks had gathered on the shores of Holy Island as the Reivers' boat grew closer. The men on board were calling and waving, their smiles unbridled as the sun began to cast its light upon the surface of the waters. At the boat's prow, Robert still held fast to his brother, speaking rapidly into his face, his eyes begging him to understand.

"Those men had been soldiers of the king once," he whispered, "but when they sailed from Blamenholm, they were men no more."

A chill rattled through Walter, and he took a great breath, casting his mind back to only a few hours ago when the sky was dark over that island.

The Reivers had assailed the looming rock of Blamenholm's outer walls, dispatching the shivering guards atop the walls with ease. Old men they had been, with wide, glassy eyes and marks of red pox around their mouths and ears. Walter had almost felt pity for the wretched creatures as he hacked at their throats, listening to their lives give way with a wheeze. Relief it had been as he had watched the last of their spindly bodies topple from the walls and be swallowed into the darkness of the island below.

It was the sound he had heard that rippled upward from the darkness behind those grim outer walls which had sent a chill haring up the back of his neck. It was not human, not even close, yet it sounded like no beast he had ever heard: a gurgling, growling rumble that had shaken the very stone on which they stood. And something, yes, some thing had moved down there in the darkness. Was it not the screech of long-cold chains and the longing rasp of saliva pulled back from teeth, the way a tethered hound baits a roasting spit?

98

The men had not stayed to discover this devilry, simply flown the walls and fled back to the boat, crossing themselves frantically, their eyes wide and pale in the ghost light from the moon above. Above them all, cast the shadow of Blamenholm keep, its face a specter that leered down with ancient, dead eyes. No cajoling, threats or insults that Walter hurled after he'd joined them on the deck could persuade them to do otherwise, and without a glance at their leader, they had cast the boat's moorings, heaving at the few oars until the crumpled prow faced away from that terrible place and back into the rising waves of the North Sea.

They had sailed the fleeting few hours of the waning night and now faced sanctity on Lindisfarne. Walter would not begrudge the men as, like Robert said, to tempt madness would beckon mutiny in.

He stared, leaning forward as Holy Isle came into view. The monks were in plain sight now, faces just visible behind their stitched cowls. From a distance, they had appeared to be waving as if in greeting, but as Walter looked upon their faces, another chill like that behind the walls of Blamenholm filled him again. He turned to stare at his brother and the men whose heads now faced behind, looking back from where they had come.

Walter was a man who had seen terror, he had stared into the eyes of soldiers who saw their own death reflected in the blade of his sword. He had glimpsed the uncomprehending fear in the eyes of those who had their homes and their lands purged by the Milburns. He saw this now in Robert's eyes and in the eyes of the monks who stood on the shores of their holy place, waving them back, back away across the sea. With a leden misery that bloomed suddenly inside his stomach, Walter turned his head to be the last to follow the gaze of his men.

Engulfing what had been open sea behind the boat, the rays of the morning sun cast their light against the colossal, curved prow of the great ship that sat, swollen and silent atop the waves behind them.

Robert Milburn whispered a prayer as the empty eye sockets of the ship's dragon-head grinned down monstrously into his own. Silent as a sea bird that rests on the crest of a wave, it moved closer, swallowing the emerging dawn. There came a creaking as its tattered, black sail caught the wind and that terrible colossus of the waves moved toward them.

17

The dawn had risen slyly into the pastel blue of early daylight by the time Martin Walker reached the port village of Seahouses. He barely registered the journey, driving in a grim trance as the pale sun rose over the flat landscape. The sleepy, white windows of the cottages and stubby line of houses that flanked the road gazed lazily at the car that roared briefly past en route to the small harbor at its mouth.

He had felt it all the way along the narrow B-roads that wound their way through the countryside from the mill cottage to this silent coastline. It was no longer a fury that whirled against the walls, but the watchful spite that had followed him as went from room to empty room to look for his family, just to see the empty spaces where they should have been, to prove it, just so he knew that he wasn't going crazy. He could feel it smirking as he climbed the stairs, its smugness as he packed a few things from the bedroom into a rucksack and its mirth as he stepped out into the rain. The mud of the churned, forest path had sucked at his boots, and he clenched his teeth as the spatter of the rain against the trees' leaves was an endless imp-like giggle. As he closed the door of the car and turned the key, he swore, silently inside some locked depths in his mind, just in case that fucker was listening, that whatever happened, that even if his bones ended up scattered to sand at the bed of that sea, he would fight.

The tiny parking lot that sat atop the short harbor, unprotected from the constant whirl of the wind from the sea, was deserted. Rows of white dwellings faced the water and a short road pointed to where the few fishing boats were docked along twin, concrete jetties.

Exiting his vehicle, Martin gasped at the bite of the cold dawn. This was where they had come only weeks ago, his children, and ridden the sea to the Farnes. Had it seen them? Had that foul place reared, snake-like across the waves and seen *him*, its own death inside *them* and coveted his flesh as its own?

Stop it, dammit! He forced his voice into the flailing edge of his mind, don't sweat the detail, get to the heart, hear its beat. How many times had he used this particular phrase during a dull board meeting? How often had he used the sentiment to tear through the endless red tape of bureaucracy to pin down a deal? But this time it was not about money, it was about his family.

The cold sea air greeted Martin with a snap of its jaws as he slammed the door of the car and jogged from the parking lot to the harbor, casting furtively for other souls exploring this bare shoreline. He saw nothing but the still black of darkened windows. He slowed his pace, pressing himself close to the sandblasted flagstones near the ghastly blue and beige of a block of apartments that rose above the harbor to a much older row of stone boatsheds with curved, wooden doors. Faded signage screwed to the uneven brickwork spoke of lifeboats and CCTV. The sea was to his left, and despite the gloom of the morning, he felt horribly exposed. Only a stubby wall separated him from the waves.

A few feet onto the jetty, past the boatsheds, the bulbous orange buoys swayed on a single blue craft bobbing gently against the stone. On the larger jetty to his left stood several fishing and tourist vessels, their hulls propped up on rusted metal feet. Martin allowed himself one fleeting glimpse across the green shifting waters into the distance. Adrenaline from a great surge of fear—or maybe excitement—made his head feel light. The brown banks of the Farne islands were just visible in the distance, and beyond them, beyond those great stacks of ancient rock, was where that ship had taken his family. There, far out to sea where nothing else dreamed to dwell, was where the great keep of Blamenholm sat, its gate open wide to welcome them inside.

Please, he thought, standing as still and as small as he could and staring back to the small vessel tied to the jetty. There had to be someone there, there just had to be.

Minutes went by and the wind picked up. Martin could feel his nose beginning to run and desperation began to rumble in his stomach, his breath came in long quivers. The harbor was completely still, save for the hiss of the sea against the walls, and Martin swallowed, his throat dry. There was no turning back now, he had never turned from anything in his life and he would not turn from this. He could feel the gaze of the island from across the sea, nothing but distance between Martin and Blamenholm's rancid leer. The raucous indigence of the gulls, bobbing lazily on the waves, were one step from cat calls.

I'm no sailor, he thought, but point a prow toward that place and hit the gas, what could be so difficult?

He crept forward, crab-like across the path to the gap in the sea wall where iron rungs were welded, leading down to the deck of the lone boat. Martin looked up again at the silent houses high on the coastline and a desolate loading bay behind the back of some shops. The only movement was in the closed lids of curtains and blinds, short arcs of condensation from the sleeping, oblivious bodies within.

The rungs were freezing on his hands as he descended the harbor wall and clambered on the damp deck of the blue boat.

With a clench of his teeth and hissing exhalation, Martin attempted to stir courage from the churning in his stomach. The fury he had felt not minutes ago was beginning to ebb, replaced with a terrible weariness that hung wetly from his limbs and forced flickering shadows scurrying from his peripheral vision.

You won't win that way. Martin almost spoke the words out loud, as a ghastly hunger wailed from the depths of his abdomen.

Keep it going, Mart. You've got it on the ropes, this is why you're like this… this is why. He breathed a ragged sigh. One of the many gulls that filled the harbor alighted clumsily a few feet in front of him. The bird was young but as big as a small dog. It wore a gray crown of feathers and beak in place of the stark adult yellow. Martin paused as the gull cocked its head and looked up at him with one blank, pearl-like eye.

Come on, Mart, it's a freaking gull, what's it gonna do? His legs locked and his stomach squeezed with terrible fear.

The gull hopped on the spot and ruffled its wings as if not certain whether to go forward or back.

"If you take one step back right now, just one, that's it," Martin mutter as the gull now extended its wings in a span that was easily four feet. Jesus Christ, if this was the youngster what sort of monster was the mom? It barked a strange, long noise and flapped, the beat of its wings sending a rotten, salty odor into Martin's nostrils. This was it.

"Get!" Martin shouted. Not shrieked, he definitely did not *shriek*, and kicked out at the gull which leaped off the side of the boat, calling again in that defiant caw.

"Home!" it seemed to yell. "Home, get home!"

Of course it did.

Legs bent, Martin crept forward along the deck, his footfalls deliberate, quiet. Around him, he could hear the hiss of the waves urging him backward, their whispers a thousand wet sneers. He closed his eyes and pictured the tight faces of men in suits who told him no, you simply cannot, the strained wrinkle in Martha's smile when he said he would be away yet again for another six months. This time it would be different because this was the last time. This was his family, the family on which he had lavished electronics and aesthetics for years as he stood in boardrooms and pored over plans. The family he had let down.

He swung himself silently from the roof of the boat onto the deck, not noticing his agility, only focused on the task in hand. A closed, white door stood before him that led into the cabin of the small boat, the cabin windows were suffused with tarpaulin, presumably to give a degree of privacy to its occupant. Martin took a deep breath and puffed out his chest slightly. He would use simple psychology, his accent and self-assurance might gain him entry. There was no need to start a commotion if he could help it.

He rapped sharply at the door, and within a minute or so the door of the boat opened slightly and a sleep-heavy face peered around it. Martin felt a pang of guilt as he looked into the confused and widening eyes of a white-bearded older man wearing a gray bobble hat and stained yellow oilskins.

"Sir," Martin addressed him, his voice horribly loud in the silence of the harbor. The man went to close the door, but Martin pushed himself into the gap and levered it open with his right elbow.

"Sir, please… I… " His throat tightened and his mind whirled, what the hell was he supposed to say?

Excuse me, sir, I need to borrow your boat and sail out to a desolate island in the middle of the North Sea to save my family. Sir, you had better sail because if I'm sure of anything, I'm sure that whatever it is that has my family will see me coming.

In the split second as he stammered for breath, the man reached into his oilskin pocket and pulled out a mobile phone; he raised the phone to his ear and pointed his other hand at Martin, raised in a "stop" signal.

Martin saw the guy's fingers clicking at one digit. Once, twice, this could be it, this could be over right now.

"Please!" Martin yelled and this time his voice was bereft of the vigor that had scared the gull. "Please. Sir." He held out his arms, palms wide. "Please, sir." He felt disgust at himself as the first few tears began coursing down his cheeks. "Please help me."

The old man lowered his phone slowly and stared at Martin, his hand still held up before him.

"Please." Martin now saw the concern in the guy's eyes turn to wary fear, the look you have when you give a homeless guy some change and he starts walking alongside you, spouting about how God has chosen you this day.

Come on, Mart, get a hold of yourself. He worked hard to quell the tears and pull his face into a controlled mask of gratitude.

"They…" he had to be so careful of his next few words. He made no move toward the man, the phone was still in his hand, his finger poised over that final nine. Martin stared around first to the right and then to the left. "Sir... they've got my family."

"Drugs?" The old man's sudden, barked accusation sounded more like a disapproving grandfather than a simple fisherman woken at dawn by some crying yank. Anger flashed through Martin for a second but was quickly quashed with relief.

"Yes," he said, quietly, trying the idea out in his head, so much better than what would sound like ravings of a madman if he told the man the truth. The guy was staring intently at him now, staring *into* him and for a lurching second Martin wanted to tell this bearded grandfather the horrible truth. For a crazy moment he wanted to fall into the man's arms and sob out the truth into his jumper that would smell of sweat and the sea, lighten the unspeakable load because he'd understand. He'd be able to help. He'd...

Stop it. Get a goddamn grip of yourself.

"My destination is Blamenholm, you know it?"

A silence hung between them and, in that moment, Martin could almost see the color draining from the man's whiskery face.

"I know that place," the man finally said, lowering his hand as well as his eyes.

"I can take you to it. But you'll kill me before I set one foot on shore." He glared at Martin through thick, tufts of eyebrow.

"Deal."

Within minutes the small fishing boat had left behind the silent harbor at Seahouses and was chugging gently east to the faint islands far in the distance.

18

Martin Walker stood atop a short ridge of rocks and faced the sea.

Behind him rose the crumbling keep of Blamenholm. He did not look, but he could feel it, squat and patient, awaiting him.

The little blue-hulled fishing boat looked already like a child's toy as it bobbed between the waves, getting smaller and smaller until it disappeared into the horizon. By the time the boat was a speck, morning had opened her puffy eyes and stared down through coils of gray cloud.

The air felt heavy, almost humid despite the wind's permanent wail, and a headache was churning between Martin's eyes. This was no place like home, God and Jesus in holy heaven, no, but the sweat pooling uncomfortably at the small of his back and the way his breath caught in his chest was a sickly tug to the summers on the other side of the Atlantic, where the roads shimmered and the trees pulsed green. Here though, there was only a fine, damp mist that moistened his face and the steady whine of the wind whipping relentlessly against the rock. It was hard to think of home as being real when he was here in this bitter place. It was getting even harder to remember home, all that mattered now was here. Now. The closer he had come to Blamenholm, the heavier this feeling became, and Martin had felt his mind rolling with the movement of the boat on the sea. He felt drunk, high even, and his thoughts were getting closed out by a dank fog. There was only one thing that mattered to him now, and that was Blamenholm and the black-sailed ship that had carried his wife and kids into its heart.

The skipper, Matty Dunn, had been scared, weak, his jagged accent dripped with fear as he told Martin about the shadows that rose from that keep, the blood-lights that hung in the sky and the howling that rode the winds around the island. He'd spoken of Blamenholm's black heart, the pit below the keep that was so dangerous, no one dared go inside. It was that way for a reason, the guy had said: *It works two ways, to keep folk out and to keep something else in.*

Trance-like, his movements slow, the cool air and the soft loll of the sea transfixing him, he began to turn into the dawn, his eyes hungrily embracing the tall walls behind which Blamenholm keep loomed.

Its walls seemed to grow from the land itself, huge clumps of white scurvy grass protruding from between the uneven chunks of ancient stone at its lower half.

He tread carefully along the vague path to the castle walls. The grass clawed spitefully at his ankles. As he approached Blamenholm keep, he saw the ridge that ran along the summit of the outer walls was worn smooth from years of salty winds gnawing across it, so it was an uneven line as if drawn by hand.

Soon enough he stood face-to-face with the gap where the outer gate cemented clumsily to the ancient rock hung open.

There was altogether something more eerie about Blamenholm in the day. The nooks and crannies that festooned its walls held tight black shadows like the squint of hundreds of eyes against the light.

The mist clung to Blamenholm like a fungus, and the twin slits of its windows glared down in a malevolent leer. The interior gates stood ahead, and as Martin came closer he could see that the chains and boards that held the place closed on their first visit had been torn down. From the fuzz inside Martin's mind swam the recollection of the doors back in the cottage, shattered where something had smashed through and taken his family.

Behind the walls, the keep reared—almost leaning back—a crumbling cobra shedding ancient scales.

To keep folk out and to keep something else in.
All manner o'things...

Everything inside Martin screamed at him to turn back. He felt his feet dragging against the land, the ground   turning from stiff rock to sodden peat. The wind pushed his eyes shut against the sight of the place that loomed closer in a great mouth-like shadow to swallow him. He clutched both handles of the rucksack he carried from the boat, put his head down, and strode onward, face already damp from a mix of sweat and the dewy mist. As he passed through the gate, he felt gooseflesh stand on his forearms and he hummed, loud, teeth clenched, blocking out the creak of rusted metal and the skeletal clink of chains as the gate closed behind him.

The sound of the wind and the crash of the sea abated swiftly. Behind the outer walls of Blamenholm, Martin Walker stood alone.

20

Martin felt an empty horror in the pit of his stomach as he had walked the thin, silent path from the gate to the door of Blamenholm's keep. He kept his eyes down in front of him, not wanting to see the spidery flickers of something that darted in and out of the thin windows and repulsive black shadows, something he was sure peered around the walls at him, its thin fingers clicking against the ancient stone. He could feel his voice coming in a low, uncontrollable moan in his throat, his lower jaw trembling as he stood in the vast expanse of that curved, cobweb-drenched hall. The door closed silently behind him, cutting off the light from outside.

Absolute silence.

Moments later the swish of the sea came murmuring through the gaps between door and the walls. There were other sounds too, fluttering and scuttling, that chilled Martin's blood as he thought of long-quiet footsteps falling predatorily against the ancient rock, drawn to the smell of blood.

It took a few minutes before he remembered the ancient trap that hung high, poised like some terrible iron spider. The damn thing was centuries old and if it fell… well, that was just about game over, thank you and goodnight. He pressed himself against the wall, the back of his head coming in contact with the jagged and slightly damp stone. He shuddered. Even touching things in the damn place was giving him the heebie-jeebies.

The curves in the ceiling and the passageways coiled upward into the bowels of the keep like the inside of a shell, and Martin could see in his minds' eye the giant, motionless coils of some ancient thing. He had to stop this. The madness was pulsing, brimming in his mind, and he could feel screams building, flashes of the last few hours were careening before him as he pressed himself against the inside of Blamenholm, the creak of nails on rotten nails as the wind filled that foul ship's black sail.

A hideous association snapped together inside Martin as he recalled Chad's third birthday. Two of the kids that had been invited had gotten into a scrap and one had thrown Jell-O at the windows. It had stuck and slithered down, he remembered the way its pink sheen had caught the light. He gave a great hiccupping sob that was swallowed hungrily by the gloomy reaches of Blamenholm's ceilings.

This was about what the place had taken from *him*.

This was about getting them back.

Blamenholm began to stir as if in answer to the desperate fury that reared inside Martin. What had begun as a rattle somewhere high, somewhere in the walls, became a steady thrumming, not of feet but of… it sounded like a hundred hands beating against solid rock, and it resonated against the curvature of the walls, bouncing in all directions. What was it Saul had said, in his hammy Gandalf voice as they had stood so close together, huddled as a family in this place?

The real genius of Blamenholm's design is that attention paid to how sound works in here. Three people descending the stairs in one of the higher towers can sound like an army to the people in the keep. No one is quite sure where they are coming from, only that they are coming.

"I'm coming!" Martin roared, tearing himself from the wall and hurling himself into one of the curved corners of the keep, feeling the damp, blunt edges of

112

stone under his fingertips as he clattered up a set of crumbling stone stairs.

His heart pounded as mocking laughter began to echo throughout the castle. All he could see was Martha, Lauren, and Chad, their faces, their smiles, their scared eyes as they waited for him to come to them, to *get home*.

Blamenholm keep has four towers, appearing from the outside as square turrets protruding from each corner, much like a classic, medieval British castle keep. Inside, however, they are towers in the loosest sense of the word. There are four spiral staircases that begin in the four corners of the keep, hacked out of the stone itself, as if the keep were some vast cave that had been created from the inside-out. With every step taken upward into the claustrophobic turrets, where the ceiling hangs unevenly with only limited crawling space, one becomes more and more aware of the intricacy of the building. The overriding impression inside the keep is as if something had been imprisoned deep amidst the lonely rock and had spent the centuries scraping space from its stony prison.

Martin climbed each of Blamenholm's four towers. The only clue to the time of day were the few tendrils of light that sputtered fleetingly into the main hall from the twin slits in the keep's face. Pitch blackness hung in the towers. Martin ascended them slowly, blindly groping through the silken, shroud-like cobwebs that clung to his hands. He moved slowly, conscious of terrible rustlings from the curved corners, telling himself over and over again that it was a bird, a draft, the sea. As he ascended each tower and reached the summit, tumbling into dank crawlspaces that contained only silence and slits in the stone from which to point a weapon, the fear began to emit a steady, humming sound he did not even know he was making. Every step downward from the empty towers, his heels sliding and scraping on the ancient rock, he could hear something sniffing at the air in front, he could feel whiskers—or were they cobwebs—brushing against his face. He hummed to block out the sound of a steady growling that grew sometimes louder, sometimes quieter, sometimes from above him, below him, or the most horrible time, when he had reached the summit of the fourth staircase and lay, shivering in the blackness of the final, empty tower, right beside him.

His eyes could not, would not, become accustomed to the blackness inside the castle *or are they shut? Do you have them shut? Are you that scared that you can't even open your eyes and look for them?*

He became aware of his humming. It wavered in his throat and broke occasionally with sobs. Beyond three feet of stone the sun shone on the waves and yet in the keep it was always night, always dark, always dead.

What was it Martha had said once? What Martha had screamed, in one of her harsh whispers that scythed the air as the children lay sleeping beneath eiderdown duvets while a fake log fire crackled silently in the cream-walled living room?

"What's inside your heart?" Her face was makeup-less, her hair kinked where she had worn it tight in a high ponytail. There had been bags under her eyes and the sight of them had infuriated him.

With gritted teeth, he had lashed an arm out to point to the piles of gift-wrapped presents, their bright ribbons reflecting the ruby glow of the lights from the

Christmas tree. Why could she not see? Why would she not see? It was his work, his fucking sweat and tears that had bought their Christmas this year and yeah, so he'd have to leave at 7 pm on Christmas day to make his flight at O'Hare, but he'd rearranged the entire fucking thing so he could be with them.

"It's a cold, empty place in there, Martin Walker." She had pointed a finger at his chest and it had stung.

High in the eaves of this vile place, so far from the golden trim and fir-tinged scent of Christmas, the stench of rotten salt accompanied the steady growl of something unspeakable somewhere deep inside. Martin felt that same pang, only this time it was not his pride that stung, it was his heart.

The sea wind sighed, and with it, Martin knew what he had to do. The fear raging through him bubbled to another vomit-inducing peak because he knew that it wasn't these high places—as empty as his heart—that he must traverse but rather the lower echelons of Blamenholm.

One hundred uneven stairs, single file, in pitch darkness. The stairwell is narrow and its ceiling is low…

It seemed like years since Saul Sage had led the Walker family inside this hateful place and spoken those words. At that very moment had Martin Walker not felt that pang in his chest around his heart? Did he not know that it would be he, descending those stairs alone? He did not speculate on how he would find those stairs. Blamenholm itself would guide him. As sure as a lobster climbs tentatively into the cage that will become its prison, clattering against the bars hopelessly scouring for a way out, Martin Walker would descend step by step, deeper and deeper, into the pit of

Blamenholm, into the cold, dark place which had once been a heart.

An empty hopelessness held Martin's heart tighter and tighter in its freezing fist as he walked the downward spiral staircase into the depths of Blamenholm. With every inch that he descended, childish terror and gloom sank deeper into the pit of his stomach. With one hand brushing the dank rock of the curved wall to keep his bearings in the inky blackness, he took each crumbling step one at a time. Nice and steady, keep it in auto-Mart... don't panic. Martin hummed to block out the idea that was pressing its tricky fingers into his mind. The passage leading downward into the earth was wide, hugely wide with a great drop in its center like a throat. Roots coiled upward like vast, knotty arteries. The idea that the stairs he inched along were mere inches wide and one wrong step would send him tumbling silently into nothing, swallowed by the darkness, consumed him.

Where are the traps? Martin thought to himself, rubbing his left thigh against the wall. The stairs felt shorter, smaller, slipperier as he went on. He waved in the blank air, feeling nothing but the darkness, withdrawing his fingers swiftly as if from the nip of sharp teeth. All he had to do was stop, turn back, return to the surface. But the steady trudge of his feet dragged him forward no matter the violent protest from his mind, no matter what his heart begged.

22.

It seemed like hours,
    Damp, black hours,
            No light from above,
                    Nor from below,
                        And
always
Something watched
        And waited.

At least he was no longer spiraling. The darkness was complete, but Martin had more of a sense of what went before him. Monolithic gray shadows that loomed and leered in and out of perspective were the only clues to indicate where he was heading. The staircase seemed straight now, passing from the throat-like maw into some sub-tunnel. There was now wall on both sides, it crumbled slightly at his touch, a ghastly cold mud-like texture wedging easily beneath his fingernails. It was above his head, too, and Martin kept his neck bent ever so slightly for the touch of that shallow ceiling sent the damn jitters through him. What was that movie which Chad had liked so much? *The Return of the King*, that part near the end where Mr. Frodo, tattered and frayed, his elven cloak crisscrossed with dirt and his blue eyes empty, dead, was climbing through those rocks.

Torech Ungol, Dad! Of course, you could count on the Chadster to know all the place names. The kid loved those damn movies.

Good old Mr. Frodo who had started off the movie with a twinkle in his eye and a smile on his face was now blank and pale, staring up at that tower where that great eye hung suspended. But it wasn't that which had sent the hairs on his arms trembling and his fingers twisting into little claws, it was that damn spider that emerged behind him. It *hung* silently behind good old Mr. Frodo, its face a black scowl, eight foul legs that reached for the little hobbit, its furry maw that oozed with inhuman malice.

It was the damn thing's silence that had gotten to him, had gotten to the both of them.

"How will I know, Dad?" Chad had stammered, his cold toes pressed up against Martin's hip as they lay in the king-size on one of the rare occasions Martin was home.

"How do I know it's not there, if I can't even hear it?"

Those words had stayed with Martin long after Martha had placated their son and coaxed him back to his bedroom. *How do I* know *it's not there?*

He gave a small cry, balling his fists under his chin like a baby, feeling sudden tears in his eyes. The ceiling dipped slightly and brushed at his hair, sending that fear rushing through him. He had to keep it together now, he could not let it get to him, had to forget how far he had come in this endless blackness, a step at a time. He could not even conceive of the ancient tons of rock that sat above him.

The stairs had ended, the path on which he moved ever onward had reached a plateau and was flat. God only knew how deep he was now beneath the keep. One foot in front of the other. The way was getting narrower, the roughly hewn walls now brushed their filth along his shoulders. He held his hands before him.

This had to lead somewhere.

And as if in answer to the scream building inside him as he pushed himself through this vile crevice in the rock, it did.

Finally, Martin emerged from the passageway into *somewhere*. The stone no longer pulled at him, and he sensed air above his head. He pulled his phone from his pocket, eyes squinting against its light, mind spinning. There was no way back now. Was it the fear of what he might see, what pale eyes would catch that light, eyes that had not seen naught but darkness for centuries, what had been lurking for generations would move its long-still limbs and crawl with dripping jaws, searching for the life that shone its light into the bowels of Blamenholm castle? Frantically, with trembling fingers, he found the flashlight app on his phone, trying not to notice that he had less than half a bar of battery left, pushed it, closing his eyes momentarily against the light.

It was huge. Huge and empty. The light emitted in a confident stream from the phone as it guzzled the remaining battery, illuminated this final room, Blamenholm's last card.

From the short reach of the phone's light, the height of the chamber could not be calculated, but it thankfully did not feel like the tunnel before. In keeping with the odd curvature of Blamenholm's upper chambers, this room was also a beguiling and disconcerting shape. From what he could make out as he shone the light before him, it was long and fairly narrow. The ground beneath his feet was softer than the rough-hewn rock of the tunnel and his feet made an eerie *clop* as he took a few furtive steps forward. The floor was wood—smooth and black with age—and he was walking along a thin gangway with rows of seats on either side of him. This felt more like a church than a dungeon, its silence almost holy but for the horror that was building inside him. A sweet odor permeated the air like some vile incense.

Martin shone the light from right to left, one hand at his mouth in awe. Rows of black, wooden benches lined the gangway on each side. The walls beyond the benches were black too, colossal planks of wood overlapping like scales. Bolted to these walls between each bench were chains, several for each bench, each set connected to a set of bones that had presumably been seated on the benches but now lay in coiled heaps on the floors, curved yellowing ribcages and skulls grinning maniacally. At the end of each set of chains were manacles, most of which lay atop the skeletal heaps. Pale forearms still dangled ghoulishly from some of the metal cuffs.

Blamenholm's dungeon was not a mere holding place or torture chamber but a ship, a dead ship whose crew sat in rows, chained to its hull to as futile passengers deep below the earth. Martin moved forward, down the middle of this vile craft, his breathing coming in huge, wheezing gulps. He stared at the rows of skeletons, some that clung pitifully to their chains, some bent forward in desperate prayers, all of them facing one way, the way his feet were carrying him, into the blackness, the way forward.

There was then a colossal sound, a rumbling from everywhere all at once. The chains gnashed like metal teeth, the very floor shook, and Martin pitched forward, his phone clattering into a pile of bones before him and its light going out. Panic seized him as he went to his knees, reaching blindly before him and grasping at one of the benches. It came again, the sound more like a roar this time, pure hate infused with the smashing sound of waves. The hull of the long-buried boat shook again, but this time he heard something else, some other sounds approaching in the blackness before him.

Behind the shuddering of the ship and the steady roar of the sea, there was something else: a sound that rattled along each vertebrae of the spine and down into his gut. It was a growl, purely predatory, but it was its accompaniment that made it all the more chilling in this unspeakable darkness: the steady pad of bipedal feet that picked through the piles of bones. It was whatever had been watching him as he had descended those terrible stairs below the keep, he knew it. It would get closer and... was that a sniff of the air that sent little sobs of pure fear burbling from between his lips? It was close and then it was far away then it was gone completely for a few seconds, up to a minute, as it too was searching.

Martin stumbled to his feet and nearly crashed over again, then he lunged forward, his ankle twisting as the sole of his foot collided with the edge of one of the benches. He held his hands before him, waving them desperately as he staggered forward.

There were screams now, *human* screams—and did that inhuman growl suddenly stop as if it, too, had heard them?

"Martha!" Martin screamed, his voice cracked and high with terror. "Lauren! Chad!"

Their screams were clearer, no, closer—if he could just find them.

He began to move through the ship, a step at a time, panting with the effort of keeping upright, both hands reaching to his sides, grasping at the rows of pew-like benches, fingers curling with revulsion as they brushed occasionally against bone. The ship was shuddering, its wooden hull creaking with the violent crashes of what could only be water pounding them. It was impossible, had to be, unless the very rock of the island itself had been somehow constructed *over* this vessel. That was impossible, it had to be. Nevertheless, the floor rocked from side to side as if riding the waves of a furious sea. The darkness was horribly disconcerting along with the ghoulish crunch of bone against wood as Blamenholm's skeletal crew slid back and forth along its floor.

"Martha! Kids!" Martin tried again, and this time his cry was quelled by the frenzied roar of water and a moaning from the hull. He pitched to one side as the ship swayed sickeningly to its left and felt the crack of brittle bones beneath his feet. But there had been something from up ahead, louder this time. He staggered, desperate to stay upright on the narrow gangway. There was a panting coming from somewhere on his right, he clenched his jaw to drown out the scream that the noise nearly sent heaving from inside him. He imagined a thick, wet, hungry tongue that had not had tasted flesh for a long, long time.

"I'm here! Come back!"

It was Lauren, her voice thick with terror, but unmistakable. The ship shuddered and groaned again but Martin heaved himself forward with great strides, he could hear Chad, too, his screams high amongst the crashing and groaning of the ship. There was a terrible chittering noise which could only be the rush of chains but was right now was the gabble of some unspeakable creature laughing at him staggering around in the dark, up and down in this empty ship of bones.

"Where the hell are you?" he screamed, falling as the boat pitched upward as if it hung on the crest of a wave. Cracking and crunching came from beneath him as he landed headlong into a pile of bones, sharp splinters of shattered ribs pressing into his legs and forearms as he heaved himself to his feet again. Another rattle of chains.

"Dad!" It was one of the kids—close this time, so close—another clatter of iron and the unmistakable *thunk* as they pulled taught against their moorings in the wall.

"Daddy! Please!"

"Jesus." Martin panted as a memory floated into his mind: The scar that curled around Saul Sage's wrist and the words he had spoken to them in the gloom of Blamnholm's keep.

I have only ventured down there once in my life.

Frantic now, he began flailing around in the dark, and his shins smashed against one of the wooden benches that reared up in front of him, sending Martin tumbling to the floor again as the boat rolled and thundered around him. The voices of his family seemed to be coming from all around him. There was a crash and he tumbled into a pile of skulls and limbs, the darkness around him became complete, and for a few seconds he had no idea which way was up and which was down. He moaned, the sound lost in the creaking of the ship, arms curled around his face, wet from tears, mucus and what was either sweat or blood, he did not know. The world went blue, then red as he struggled to remain conscious. Things were slowing down, the roar of the sea became a strangled gargle.

"No!" he croaked, thrusting his arms out in front of him and catching hold of one of the dangling chains. Its manacle thankfully did not contain a wrist and he heaved himself upright, swaying, clutching at the chain like the pole of a whirling carousel. Tentatively now, using one hand to feel his way along the wall and the other holding the chain, he began moving. As the chain pulled taught, he reached into the blackness for the next one and pulled at that, taking the slack and keeping him moving. The panting sound was thankfully quiet for now and the whisper of soft feet on the floor was also silent. He strained his ears against the roaring of the sea for the voices of his family, but then he saw something that filled him with blessed relief.

Light.

It was fleeting, a flickering, bluish glow which was extinguished sporadically from view by the movement of the ship, but it was there. Martin staggered forward, the ancient chains clasped in both hands.

"Lauren!" he yelled. "Chad!"

And there was the growling, loud, only feet behind him. He heard crashing as feet kicked aside the bones that littered the rolling floor and panting, ravenous with a repulsive, throaty gargle to it now. Whatever was making the noise had held off for this long, but now it could no longer contain itself. It was coming.

"Daddy!"

The boat reared. Was that the sound of scrabbling claws trying to grip the ancient wood? The light up ahead was only a few rows before him, and Martin, guided only by desperation, chanced a glance behind him, in spite of the darkness.

A pair of ice-blue eyes shone ten feet behind him.

He gave an involuntary cry and leaped forward toward the light, reaching into the dark at his feet and hurling what felt like a ribcage behind him, a flailing skeletal hand clawing at his cheek, drawing a hot welt of pain. He heard another scraping of claws on wood, a crash, and the eyes disappeared.

Martin skidded around one of the benches as the boat tipped forward this time and fell, gasping to the floor beside the source of the flickering light.

It was Lauren, pale and wide-eyed, her hair tousled in a damp mane around her head. She was crouched, knees high beside a thick, horizontal wooden pillar, her phone, the source of the illumination, in her hand. Chad was beside her, his phone held up before him. They pressed against each other, shoulder to shoulder, their faces in the dim phone light looking like a pair of Victorian street-urchins.

It was them, finally, in the flesh, but there was something wrong. Lauren and Chad stared up at their father, eyes widening and mouths opening in horror. The boat rumbled, sending Martin sliding backward and away from them. The children hollered in unison, their phone lights flickered as they scrambled to their feet.

What was wrong? Did they not recognize their father?

A sudden rage reared in Martin and he threw himself forward, back to where his children now stood. Chad was cowering behind his sister and Lauren had her shoulders thrown back, her face thunderous and protective. She turned her phone toward her father and the light dazzled him, turning, sending his arm instinctively over his eyes.

"Come on!" Martin bawled, splaying his hands wide, turning his face from the light. "Come to me!"

There was an eerie stillness, the roar of the water diminished slightly, and it was as if Blamenholm was now watching, sneering down at him, a voyeur.

The damn phone light was still horribly dazzling after the constant darkness of the dungeon, it was infuriatingly impossible to look up at them. Chad shrieked as Martin staggered a few steps forward, his hand reaching out. With gritted teeth, he looked up into the glare. The kids had moved backward, away from him, pressing themselves desperately into the curve of the boat's hull.

"Come on," he could barely croak, tears on his cheeks. "It's me. It's *me*."

"Get away from them!" the scream came from the other side of the ship and Martin whirled around. Had that been the growling again, from somewhere behind him, the *pat-pat* of paws on the wood?

Another blue phone light from the other side of the gangway; it waved frantically, and his wife's voice was hard, defiant.

"Take me!" she screeched. "Take me instead!"

And in this sudden lull of the boat's movement, he looked slowly from his children to his wife. Like the crumpled masses of bones that littered the hull of Blamenholm, his family were attached by one wrist each to the ship's hull. The sight of the blackened metal manacles drove a chill deep into the pit of his stomach. The growling and panting was close, so close now, almost upon him but now it did not matter. Now something had loosened at the bed of his mind and floated to the surface sifting the silt of memory.

"Look at yourself." Martha was sobbing now, shining the light from her phone at her husband's chest.

He stared down at his own body in the dim light; fur cloaked him, matted with blood, and an axe hung from his hand. That's when the laughter came, the same laughter that sent him fleeing from the mill cottage in pursuit of the black ship of Blamenholm. It echoed from all around, reverberating around the ship. Deep, ancient and insane.

Nausea now and the need to shit squeezed at his bowels with cruel fingers. Had he been wearing this since he had sailed for the island? As if in answer, a fleeting memory prickled at the base of his skull; pacing, pacing, tearing through the woods, his feet, *his paws* light against the mud.

"No!" Martin screamed, but now he heard his voice for what it was, a guttural, canine roar. More of Saul's words came floating back to him.

Legend says they used the fortress to awaken the berserkers; that they lost their minds, that they became "berserk" in the fortress of Blamenholm...

Hunger, a colossal, tearing hunger nearly doubled him over with its force. His mouth filled with saliva and he gave another ear-splitting roar that masked the screaming of his family. He resisted with every inch of his being but like a vessel filling with water, he felt the bloodlust spilling over inside.

This was not Blamenholm's heart.

Blamenholm had no heart.

All around him rose the glowing blue of crazed, canidae eyes. The growls were like the rumbling of a vast stomach, for this is what this place was.

Before the lights of the phones went out, the sight of Saul's curling scar around his wrist rose in Martin Walker's mind. Accompanying the cruel shards of laughter that rattled down from the inside of Blamenholm came something Saul had said.

I have only ever ventured down there once.

Deep below the keep, where there could be only misery, Blamenholm fell silent once again.

On February 5th 2012, *North East Tonight*, an English regional news program, ran a short report on an island that had disappeared beneath the sea. It was speculated that the rise in sea level had been the catalyst for the sinking of Blamenholm: approximately seven acres of sloping, bare rock topped by a squat stone castle situated approximately seventeen miles from the Northumberland coast. The reporter, Helen Pearson, commented on the fact that the majority of people in the region, let alone anywhere else, did not know of the island's existence.

"Upstaged by the wildlife sanctuary and natural beauty of the Farne Islands, Blamenholm disappeared beneath the waves without so much as a goodbye."

The report then cut to an aged, unnamed scholar standing within what appeared to be the archival basement of a university. In a lilting North-East accent, the scholar hammily read a passage from a yellowed manuscript, protected within a transparent plastic tablet.

"In this year, dark portends followed the plague of the heathen men over the Northumbrian seas. Black ships of bone rode the waves, and the skies over Holy Island were black with carrion birds. There followed great fury across the lands where brother turned on brother as Lindisfarne burned before them."

The scholar went on to discuss a rare and speculative theory amongst local historians, that the Norsemen who raided and destroyed the Holy Island of Lindisfarne did not sail directly from Scandinavia, instead, they garrisoned at the uninhabited island of

Blamenholm where a secret fortress had been constructed.

"The name 'Blamenholm' comes from the Old Norse term for 'black men,' -*holm* usually being associated with islands. The *Blámmen* were the Viking warriors and probably gave the fortress the name themselves to strike fear into their enemies and keep people away."

"There are accounts from the writings of Bede," the scholar went on, "that the prisoners of the Viking raiders were taken to Blamenholm where they were abandoned. Mainly women and children were left to wander the lonely walls of the fortress or try their luck in the freezing waters of the North Sea. These were dark, superstitious times, and it is claimed by some that warrior cults would give sacrifice to whatever dwelled there to bring them prosperity and riches when times were hard."

"Blamenholm," the reporter said, "has had its fair share of tragedy, both in its history and today."

The screen filled with blurry artists' impressions of the island.

Pearson's report continued with a more downbeat tone, explaining that, since the abandonment of the castle by its former owner, and his subsequent hospitalization, no one had cared to restore the building or even discover more about its rich history. A lonely, grim looking place, surrounded by a maze of treacherous rocks, it served little purpose so far out to sea. Its restoration would be an expensive, private investment which would take a great deal of time.

"According to sources," Pearson's voice became grim, "there was interest in the island from missing business tycoon Martin Walker of the failing Gateway resorts in the USA. Mr. Walker even went so far as to fly his family out to the North East to visit the place before he, his wife, and two children simply disappeared."

A picture of an unsmiling, bearded man filled the screen for a few seconds.

"Local fisherman Matthew Dunn and his boat, *Triumph*, remain missing as well. It is unknown if the Walkers were passengers on Dunn's craft, of if these disappearances are otherwise connected. The coast guard and Northumbria police are investigating."

A garish, airbrushed photograph of the Walkers filled the screen: Martha, Chad, and Lauren sat together on a sofa, smiling up at the camera while their father, also grinning bent over the back, head just above them, his arms encircling his family in a hug.

"Maybe it's for the best," was Pearson's parting comment, "that we, at last, say goodbye to Blamenholm."

A final shot remained on the screen: slate-blue water, rippled with waves where Blamenholm had once stood. There was silence for a few seconds before the report made its transition to local sports results, as if to contemplate the family that had paid a visit to that lonely island in the North Sea.

And never returned home.

Acknowledgements

Gratitude must be expressed to those without whom *The Black Land* would have laid unfinished on the cold, dark slab of my hard drive:

Ian Richards, who breathed life back into the initial draft and whose invaluable critique kept me going all the way to the end. I appreciate it, mate.

Richard and Paula Disley who have staunchly supported my writing, regardless of its quality.

Lancaster University Writers' Guild, Richard Dawson, Jex Collyer, the bemused staff at Seahouses Tourist Information for answering my questions, Geoff and the rest of *Blood Bound Books* staff for believing in Blamenholm and, of course, my family: Jill, Harry, and Cobweb Wesolowski.

ABOUT THE AUTHOR

MJ Wesolowski, based in Newcastle-Upon-Tyne, UK, has had short stories published in places such as *Ethereal Tales* and the *Midnight Movie Creature Feature* anthology. His dark comedy production, *Suckers,* raised money for the SOPHIE fund (Stamp Out Prejudice, Hatred and Intolerance Everywhere). *The Black Land* is his debut novella.

46148110R00085

Printed in Poland
by Amazon Fulfillment
Poland Sp. z o.o., Wrocław